IN THE ARENA: STORIES OF POLITICAL LIFE.
[NEW YORK-1913]

Published @ 2017 Trieste Publishing Pty Ltd

ISBN 9780649611737

In the Arena: Stories of Political Life. [New York-1913] by Booth Tarkington

Edited by Trieste Publishing Pty Ltd.
Cover @ 2017

www.triestepublishing.com

BOOTH TARKINGTON

IN THE ARENA: STORIES OF POLITICAL LIFE. [NEW YORK-1913]

 Trieste

THE CONVERSION OF THE SENATOR FROM STACKPOLE

IN THE
ARENA

Stories
of Political
Life

BOOTH
TARKINGTON

ILLUSTRATED BY A. I. KELLER, POWER
O'MALLEY AND J. J. GOULD

GARDEN CITY   NEW YORK
DOUBLEDAY, PAGE & COMPANY
1913

To My Father

CONTENTS

PART II.

"IN THE FIRST PLACE"

The old-timer, a lean, retired pantaloon, sitting with loosely slippered feet close to the fire, thus gave of his wisdom to the questioning student:

"*Looking back upon it all, what we most need 'in politics' is more good men. Thousands of good men* ARE *in; and they need the others who are not in. More would come if they knew how* MUCH *they are needed. The dilettantes of the clubs who have so easily abused me, for instance, all my life, for being a ward-worker, these and those other reformers who write papers about national corruption when they don't know how their own wards are swung, probably aren't so useful as they might be. The exquisite who says that politics is 'too dirty a business for a gentleman to meddle with' is like the woman who lived in the parlour and complained that the rest of her family kept the other rooms so dirty that she never went into them.*

"There are many thousands of young men belonging to what is for some reason called the 'best class,' who would like to be 'in politics' if they could begin high enough up — as ambassadors, for instance. That is, they would like the country to do something for them, though they wouldn't put it that way. A young man of this sort doesn't know how much he'd miss if his wishes were gratified. For my part, I'd hate not to have begun at the beginning of the game.

"I speak of it as a game," the old gentleman went on, "and in some ways it is. That's where the fun of it comes in. Yet, there are times when it looks to me more like a series of combats, hand-to-hand fights for life, and fierce struggles between men and strange powers. You buy your newspaper and that's your ticket to the amphitheatre. But the distance is hazy and far; there are clouds of dust and you can't see clearly. To make out just what is going on you ought to get down in the arena yourself. Once you're in it, the view

you'll have and the fighting that will come your way will more than repay you. Still, I don't think we ought to go in with the idea of being repaid.

"It seems an odd thing to me that so many men feel they haven't any time for politics; can't put in even a little, trying to see how their cities (let alone their states and the country) are run. When we have a war, look at the millions of volunteers that lay down everything and answer the call of the country. Well, in politics, the country needs ALL the men who have any patriotism — NOT to be seeking office, but to watch and to understand what is going on. It doesn't take a great deal of time; you can attend to your business and do that much, too. When wrong things are going on and all the good men understand them, that is all that. is needed. The wrong things stop going on."

BOSS GORGETT

I GUESS I've been what you might call kind of an assistant boss pretty much all my life; at least, ever since I could vote; and I was something of a ward-heeler even before that. I don't suppose there's any way a man of my disposition could have put in his time to less advantage and greater cost to himself. I've never got a thing by it, all these years, not a job, not a penny — nothing but injury to my business and trouble with my wife. *She* begins going for me, first of every campaign.

Yet I just can't seem to keep out of it. It takes a hold on a man that I never could get away from; and when I reach my second childhood and the boys have turned me out, I reckon I'll potter along trying to look knowing and secretive, like the rest of the has-beens, letting on as if I still had a place inside. Lord, if I'd put in the energy at

my business that I've frittered away on small politics! But what's the use thinking about it?"

Plenty of men go to pot horse-racing and stock
gambling; and I guess this has just been my way
of working off some of my nature in another fashion. There's a good many like me, too; not out for
office or contracts, nor anything that you can put
your finger on in particular — nothing except the
game. Of course, it's a pleasure, knowing you've
got more influence than some, but I believe the
most you ever get out of it is in being able to help
your friends, to get a man you like a job, or a good
contract, something he wants, when he needs it.

I tell you *then's* when you feel satisfied, and
your time don't seem to have been so much
thrown away. You go and buy a higher-priced
cigar than you can afford, and sit and smoke it
with your feet out in the sunshine on your porch
railing, and watch your neighbour's children playing in their yard; and they look mighty nice to you;
and you feel kind, and as if everybody else was.

But that wasn't the way I felt when I helped to
hand over to a reformer the nomination for

mayor; then it was just selfish desperation and nothing else. We had to do it. You see, it was this way: the other side had had the city for four terms, and, naturally, they'd earned the name of being rotten by that time. Big Lafe Gorgett was their best. "Boss Gorgett," of course our papers called him when they went for him, which was all the time; and pretty considerable of a man he was, too. Most people that knew him liked Lafe. I did. But he got a bad name, as they say, by the end of his fourth term as Mayor — and who wouldn't? Of course, the cry went up all round that he and his crowd were making a fat thing out of it, which wasn't so much the case as that Lafe had got to depending on humouring the gamblers and the brewers for campaign funds and so forth. In fact, he had the reputation of running a disorderly town, and the truth is, it *was* too wide open.

But *we* hadn't been much better when we'd had it, before Lafe beat us and got in; and everybody remembered that. The "respectable element" wouldn't come over to us strong enough

for anybody we could pick of our own crowd; and
so, after trying it on four times, we started in to
play it another way, and nominated Farwell
Knowles, who was already running on an independent ticket, got out by the reform and purity
people. That is: we made him a fusion candidate,
hoping to find some way to control him later.
We'd never have done it if we hadn't thought it
was our only hope. Gorgett was too strong, and
he handled the darkeys better than any man I
ever knew. He had an organization for it which
we couldn't break; and the coloured voters really
held the balance of power with us, you know, as
they do so many other places near the same size.
They were getting pretty well on to it, too, and
cost more every election. Our best chance seemed
to be in so satisfying the "law-and-order" people
that they'd do something to counterbalance this
vote — which they never did.

Well, sir, it was a mighty curious campaign.
There never really was a day when we could tell
where we stood, for certain. As anybody knows,
the "better element" can't be depended on.

There's too many of 'em forget to vote, and if the weather isn't just right they won't go to the polls. Some of 'em won't go anyway — act as if they looked down on politics; say it's only helping one boodler against another. So your true aristocrat won't vote for either. The real truth is, he don't *care*. Don't care as much about the management of his city, State, and country as about the way his club is run. Or he's ignorant about the whole business, and what between ignorance and indifference the worse and smarter of the two rings gets in again and old Mr. Aristocrat gets soaked some more on his sewer assessments. *Then* he'll holler like a stabbed hand-organ; but he'll keep on talking about politics being too low a business for a gentleman to mix in, just the same!

Somebody said a pessimist is a man who has a choice of two evils, and takes both. There's your man that don't vote.

And the best-dressed wards are the ones that fool us oftenest. We're always thinking they'll do something, and they don't. But we thought, when we took Farwell Knowles, that we had 'em

at last. Fact is, they did seem stirred up, too.
They called it a "moral victory" when we were
forced to nominate Knowles to have any chance
of beating Gorgett. That was because it was *their*
victory.

Farwell Knowles was a young man, about
thirty-two, an editorial writer on the *Herald*, an
independent paper. I'd known him all his life,
and his wife — too, a mighty sweet-looking lady
she was. I'd always thought Farwell was kind of a
dreamer, and too excitable; he was always reading papers to literary clubs, and on the speechmaking side he wasn't so bad — he liked it; but
he hadn't seemed to me to know any more about
politics and people than a royal family would. He
was always talking about life and writing about
corruption, when, all the time, so it struck me, it
was only books he was really interested in; and he
saw things along book lines. Of course he was a
tin god, politically.

He was for "stern virtue" only, and everlast-
ingly lashed compromise and temporizing; called
politicians all the elegant hard names there are,

in every one of his editorials, especially Lafe Gorgett, whom he'd never seen. He made mighty free with Lafe, referred to him habitually as "Boodler Gorgett", and never let up on him from one year's end to another.

I was against our adopting him, not only for our own sakes — because I knew he'd be a hard man to handle — but for Farwell's too. I'd been a friend of his father's, and I liked his wife — everybody liked his wife. But the boys overruled me, and I had to turn in and give it to him.

Not without a lot of misgivings, you can be sure. I had one little experience with him right at the start that made me uneasy and got me to thinking he was what you might call too literary, or theatrical, or something, and that he was more interested in being things than doing them. I'd been aware, ever since he got back from Harvard, that *I* was one of his literary interests, so to speak. He had a way of talking to me in a quizzical, condescending style, in the belief that he was drawing me out, the way you talk to some old bookpeddler in your office when you've got nothing to

do for a while; and it was easy to see he regarded
me as a "character" and thought he was studying me. Besides, he felt it his duty to study the
wickedness of politics in a Parkhurstian fashion,
and I was one of the lost.

One day, just after we'd nominated him, he
came to me and said he had a friend who wanted
to meet me. Asked me couldn't I go with him
right away. It was about five in the afternoon; I
hadn't anything to do and said, "Certainly,"
thinking he meant to introduce me to some friend
of his who thought I'd talk politics with him. I
took that for granted so much that I didn't
ask a question, just followed along up street,
talking weather. He turned in at old General
Buskirk's, and may I be shot if the person he
meant wasn't Buskirk's daughter, Bella! He'd
brought me to call on a girl young enough to be
my daughter. Maybe you won't believe I felt like
a fool!

I knew Buskirk, of course (he didn't appear),
but I hadn't seen Bella since she was a child.
She'd been "highly educated" and had been liv-

ing abroad a good deal, but I can't say that my
visit made me *for* her — not very strong. She was
good-looking enough, in her thinnish, solemn
way, but it seemed to me she was kind of over-
dressed and too grand. You could see in a minute
that she was intense and dreamy and theatrical
with herself and superior, like Farwell; and I
guess I thought they thought they'd discovered
they were "kindred souls," and that each of them
understood (without saying it) that both of them
felt that Farwell's lot in life was a hard one because Mrs. Knowles wasn't up to him. Bella gave
him little, quiet, deep glances, that seemed to help
her play the part of a person who understood
everything — especially him, and reverenced
greatness — especially his. I remember a fellow
who called the sort of game it struck me they were
carrying on "those soully flirtations."

Well, sir, I wasn't long puzzling over why he
had brought *me* up there. It stuck out all over,
though they didn't know it, and would have been
mighty astonished to think that I saw. It was in
their manner, in her condescending ways with

me, in her assumption of serious interest, and in his going through the trick of "drawing me out," and exhibiting me to her. I'll have to admit that these young people viewed me in the light of a "character." That was the part Farwell had me there to play.

I can't say I was too pleased with the notion, and I was kind of sorry for Mrs. Knowles, too. I'd have staked a good deal that my guess was right, for instance: that Farwell had gone first to this girl for her congratulations when he got the nomination, instead of to his wife; and that she felt — or pretended she felt — a soully sympathy with his ambitions; that she wanted to be, or to play the part of, a woman of affairs, and that he talked over everything he knew with her. I imagined they thought they were studying political reform together, and she, in her novel-reading way, wanted to pose to herself as the brilliant lady diplomat, kind of a Madam Roland advising statesmen, or something of that sort. And I was there as part of their political studies, an object-lesson, to bring her "more closely in touch" (as Farwell would say) with the realities he had to contend with. I was one of the "evils of politics," because I knew how to control a few wards, and get out the darkey vote almost as well as Gorgett. Gorgett would have been better, but Farwell couldn't very easily get at him.

I had to sit there for a little while, of course, like a ninny between them; and I wasn't the more comfortable because I thought Knowles looked like a bigger fool than I did. Bella's presence seemed to excite him to a kind of exaltation; he had a dark flush on his face and his eyes were large and shiny.

I got out as soon as I could, naturally, wondering what my wife would say if she knew; and while I was fumbling around among the knick-knacks and fancy things in the hall for my hat and coat, I heard Farwell get up and cross the room to a chair nearer Bella, and then she said, in a sort of pungent whisper, that came out to me distinctly:

"My knight!" That's what she called him. "My knight!" That's what she said.

I don't know whether I was more disgusted with myself for hearing, or with old Buskirk who spent his whole time frittering around the club library, and let his daughter go in for the sort of soulliness she was carrying on with Farwell Knowles.

Trouble in our ranks began right away. Our nominee knew too much, and did all the wrong things from the start; he began by antagonizing most of our old wheel-horses; he wouldn't consult with us, and advised with his own kind. In spite of that, we had a good organization working for him, and by a week before election I felt pretty confident that our show was as good as Gorgett's. It looked like it would be close.

Just about then things happened. We had dropped onto one of Lafe's little tricks mighty smartly. We got one of his heelers fixed (of course we usually tried to keep all that kind of work dark from Farwell Knowles), and this heeler showed the whole business up for a consideration. There was a precinct certain to be strong for Knowles, where the balloting was to take place

in the office-room of a hook-and-ladder company.
In the corner was a small closet with one shelf,
high up toward the ceiling. It was in the good old
free and easy Hayes and Wheeler times, and
when the polls closed at six o'clock it was planned
that the election officers should set the ballot-box
up on this shelf, lock the closet door, and go out
for their suppers, leaving one of each side to
watch in the room so that nobody could open the
closet-door with a pass-key and tamper with the
ballots before they were counted. Now, the ceiling over the shelf in the closet wasn't plastered,
and it formed, of course, part of the flooring in
the room above. The boards were to be loosened
by a Gorgett man upstairs, as soon as the box
was locked in; he would take up a piece of plank-
ing — enough to get an arm in — and stuff the
box with Gorgett ballots till it grunted. Then he
would replace the board and slide out. Of course,
when they began the count our people would know
there was something wrong, but they would be
practically up against it, and the precinct would
be counted for Gorgett.

They brought the heeler up to me, not at headquarters (I was city chairman) but at a hotel
room I'd hired as a convenient place for the more
important conferences and to keep out of the
way of every Tom-Dick-and-Harry grafter.
Bob Crowder, a ward committee-man, brought
him up and stayed in the room, while the fellow — his name was Genz — went over the
whole thing.

"What do you think of it?" says Bob, when
Genz finished. "Ain't it worth the money? I declare, it's so neat and simple and so almighty
smart besides, I'm almost ashamed some of our
boys hadn't thought of it for us."

I was just opening my mouth to answer, when
there was a signal knock at the door and a young
fellow we had as a kind of watcher in the next
room (opening into the one I used) put his head
in and said Mr. Knowles wanted to see me.

"Ask him to wait a minute," said I, for I didn't
want him to know anything about Genz. "I'll be
there right away."

Then came Farwell Knowles's voice from the

other room, sharp and excited. " I believe I'll not wait," says he. "I'll come in there now!"

And that's what he did, pushing by our watcher before I could hustle Genz into the hall through an outer door, though I tried to. There's no denying it looked a little suspicious.

Farwell came to a dead halt in the middle of the room.

"I know that person!" he said, pointing at Genz, his brow mighty black. "I saw him and Crowder sneaking into the hotel by the back way, half an hour ago, and I knew there was some devilish — "

"Keep your shirt on, Farwell," said I.

He was pretty hot. "I'll be obliged to you," he returned, "if you'll explain what you're doing here in secret with this low hound of Gorgett's. Do you think you can play with me the way you do with your petty committee-men? If you do, I'll *show* you! You're not dealing with a child, and I'm not going to be tricked or sold out of this elec — "

I took him by the shoulders and sat him down

hard on a cane-bottomed chair. "That's a dirty thought," said I, "and if you knew enough to be responsible I reckon you'd have to account for it. As it is — why, I don't care whether you apologize or not."

He weakened right away, or, at least, he saw his mistake. "Then won't you give me some explanation," he asked, in a less excitable way, "why are you closeted here with a notorious member of Gorgett's ring?"

"No," said I, "I won't."

"Be careful," said he. "This won't look well in print."

That was just so plumb foolish that I began to laugh at him; and when I got to laughing I couldn't keep up being angry. It *was* ridiculous, his childishness and suspiciousness. Right there was where I made my mistake.

"All right," says I to Bob Crowder, giving way to the impulse. "He's the candidate. Tell him."

"Do you mean it?" asks Bob, surprised.

"Yes. Tell him the whole thing."

So Bob did, helped by Genz, who was more or

less sulky, of course; and is wasn't long till I saw how stupid I'd been. Knowles went straight up in the air.

"I knew it was a dirty business, politics," he said, jumping out of his chair, "but I didn't *realize* it before. And I'd like to know," he went on, turning to me, "how you learn to sit there so calmly and listen to such iniquities. How do you dull your conscience so that you can do it? And what course do you propose to follow in the matter of this confession?"

"Me?" I answered. "Why, I'm going to send supper in to our fellows, and the box'll never see that closet. The man upstairs may get a little tired. I reckon the laugh's on Gorgett; it's his scheme and — "

Farwell interrupted me; his face was outrageously red. "*What!* You actually mean you hadn't intended to expose this infamy?"

"Steady," I said. I was getting a little hot, too, and talked more than I ought. "Mr. Genz here has our pledge that he's not given away, or he'd never have — "

"*Mister* Genz!" sneered Farwell. "*Mister* Genz has your pledge, has he? Allow me to tell you that I represent the people, the *honest* people, in this campaign, and that the people and I have made no pledges to *Mister* Genz. You've paid the scoundrel — "

"*Here!*" says Genz.

"The scoundrel!" Farwell repeated, his voice rising and rising, "paid him for his information, and I tell you by that act and your silence on such a matter you make yourself a party to a conspiracy."

"Shut the transom," says I to Crowder.

"*I'm* under no pledge, I say," shouted Farwell, "and I do not compound felonies. You're not conducting my campaign. I'm doing that, and I don't conduct it along such lines. It's precisely the kind of fraud and corruption that I intend to stamp out in this town, and this is where I begin to work."

"How?" said I.

"You'll see — and you'll see soon! The penitentiaries are built for just this — "

"*Sh, sh!*" said I, but he paid no attention.

"They say Gorgett owns the Grand Jury," he went on. "Well, let him! Within a week I'll be mayor of this town — and Gorgett's Grand Jury won't outlast his defeat very long. By his own confession this man Genz is party to a conspiracy with Gorgett, and you and Crowder are witnesses to the confession. I'll see that you have the pleasure of giving your testimony before a Grand Jury of determined men. Do you hear me? And to-morrow afternoon's *Herald* will have the whole infamous story to the last word. I give you my solemn oath upon it!"

All three of us, Crowder, Genz, and I, sprang to our feet. We were considerably worked up, and none of us said anything for a minute or so, just looked at Knowles.

"Yes, you're a little shocked," he said. "It's always shocking to men like you to come in contact with honesty that won't compromise. You needn't talk to me; you can't say anything that would change me to save your lives. I've taken my oath upon it, and you couldn't alter me a hair's breadth if you burned me at a slow fire. **Light, light,** that's what you need, the light of day and publicity! I'm going to clear this town of fraud, and if Gorgett don't wear the stripes for this my name's not Farwell Knowles! He'll go over the road, handcuffed to a deputy, before three months are gone. Don't tell me I'm injuring *you* and the party by it. Pah! It will give me a thousand more votes. I'm not exactly a child, my friends! On my honour, the whole thing will be printed in to-morrow's paper!"

"For God's sake — " Crowder broke out, but Knowles cut him off.

"I bid you good-afternoon," he said, sharply. We all started toward him, but before we'd got half across the room he was gone, and the door slammed behind him.

Bob dropped into a chair; he was looking considerably pale; I guess I was, too, but Genz was ghastly.

"Let me out of here," he said in a sick voice. "Let me out of here!"

"Sit down!" I told him.

"Just let me out of here," he said again. And before I could stop him, he'd gone, too, in a blind hurry.

Bob and I were left alone, and not talking any.

Not for a while. Then Bob said: "Where do you reckon he's gone?"

"Reckon who's gone?"

"Genz."

"To see Lafe."

"What?"

"Of course he has. What else can he do? He's gone up any way. The best he can do is to try to square himself a little by owning up the whole thing. Gorgett will know it all any way, to-morrow afternoon, when the *Herald* comes out."

"I guess you're right," said Bob. "We're done up along with Gorgett; but I believe that idiot's right, he won't lose votes by playing hob with *us*. What's to be done?"

"Nothing," I answered. "You can't head Far-well off. It's all my fault, Bob."

"Isn't there any way to get hold of him? A

crazy man could see that his best friend couldn't *beg* it out of him, and that he wouldn't spare any of us; but don't you know of some bludgeon we could hang up over him?"

"Nothing. It's up to Gorgett."

"Well," said Bob, "Lafe's mighty smart, but it looks like God-help-Gorgett now!"

Well, sir, I couldn't think of anything better to do than to go around and see Gorgett; so, after waiting long enough for Genz to see him and get away, I went. Lafe was always cool and slow; but I own I expected to find him flustered, and was astonished to see right away that he wasn't. He was smoking, as usual, and wearing his hat, as he always did, indoors and out, sitting with his feet upon his desk, and a pleasant look of contemplation on his face.

"Oh," says I, "then Genz hasn't been here?"

"Yes," says he, "he has. I reckon you folks have 'most spoiled Genz's usefulness for me."

"You're taking it mighty easy," I told him.

"Yep. Isn't it all in the game? What's the use of getting excited because you've blocked us on one precinct? We'll leave that closet out of our calculations, that's all."

"Almighty Powers, I don't mean *that!* Didn't Genz tell you — "

"About Mr. Knowles and the *Herald?* Oh, yes," he answered, knocking the ashes off his cigar quietly. "And about the thousand votes he'll gain? Oh, yes. And about incidentally showing you and Crowder up as bribing Genz and promising to protect him — making your methods public? Oh, yes. And about the Grand Jury? Yes, Genz told me. And about me and the penitentiary. Yes, he told me. Mr. Knowles is a rather excitable young man. Don't you think so?"

"Well?"

"Well, what's the trouble?"

"Trouble!" I said. "I'd like to know what you're going to do?"

"What's Knowles going to do?"

"He's sworn to expose the whole deal, as you've just told me you knew; one of the preliminaries to having us all up before the next Grand

Jury and sending you and Genz over the road, that's all!"

Gorgett laughed that old, fat laugh of his, tilting farther back, with his hands in his pockets and his eyes twinkling under his last summer's straw hat-brim.

"He can't hardly afford it, can he," he drawled, "he being the representative of the law and order and purity people? They're mighty sensitive, those folks. A little thing turns 'em."

"I don't understand," said I.

"Well, I hardly reckoned you would," he returned. "But I expect if Mr. Knowles wants it warm all round, *I'm* willing. We may be able to do some of the heating up, ourselves."

This surprised me, coming from him, and I felt pretty sore. "You mean, then," I said, "that you think you've got a line on something our boys have been planning — like the way we got onto the closet trick — and you're going to show *us* up because we can't control Knowles; that you hold that over me as a threat unless I shut him up? Then I tell you plainly I know I can't shut him

up, and you can go ahead and do us the worst you
can."

"Whatever little tricks I may or may not have
discovered," he answered, "that isn't what I
mean, though I don't know as I'd be above making such a threat if I thought it was my only way
to keep out of the penitentiary. I know as well as
you do that such a threat would only give Knowles
pleasure. He'd take the credit for forcing me to
expose you, and he's convinced that everything
of that kind he does makes him solider with the
people and brings him a step nearer this chair I'm
sitting in, which he regards as a step itself to the
governorship and Heaven knows what not. He
thinks he's detached himself from you and your
organization till he stands alone. *That* boy's head
was turned even before you fellows nominated
him. He's a wonder. I've been noticing him long
before he turned up as a candidate, and I believe
the great surprise of his life was that John the
Baptist didn't precede and herald *him*. Oh, no,
going for you wouldn't stop him — not by a
thousand miles. It would only do him good."

"Well, what *are* you going to do? Are you going to see him?"

"No, sir!" Lafe spoke sharply.

"Well, well! What?"

"I'm not bothering to run around asking audiences of Farwell Knowleses; you ought to know that!"

"Given it up?"

"Not exactly. I've sent a fellow around to talk to him."

"What use will that be?"

Gorgett brought his feet down off the desk with a bang.

"*Then* he can come to see *me*, if he wants to. D'you think I've been fool enough not to know what sort of man I was going up against? D'you think that, knowing him as I do, I've not been ready for something of this kind? And that's all you'll get out of *me*, this afternoon!"

And it was all I did.

It may have been about one o'clock, that night, or perhaps a little earlier, as I lay tossing about,

unable to sleep because I was too much disturbed in my mind — too angry with myself — when
there came a loud, startling ring at the front-door
bell. I got up at once and threw open a window
over the door, calling out to know what was
wanted.

"It's I," said a voice I didn't know — a queer,
hoarse voice. "Come down."

"Who's 'I'?" I asked.

"Farwell Knowles," said the voice. "Let me
in!"

I started, and looked down.

He was standing on the steps where the light of
a street-lamp fell on him, and I saw even by the
poor glimmer that something was wrong; he was
white as a dead man. There was something wild
in his attitude; he had no hat, and looked all mixed-up and disarranged.

"Come down — come down!" he begged
thickly, beckoning me with his arm.

I got on some clothes, slipped downstairs without wakening my wife, lit the hall light, and took
him into the library. He dropped in a chair with a

quick breath like a sob, and when I turned from lighting the gas I was shocked by the change in him since afternoon. I never saw such a look before. It was like a rat you've seen running along the gutter side of the curbstone with a terrier after it.

"What's the matter, Farwell?" I asked.

"Oh, my God!" he whispered.

"What's happened?"

"It's hard to tell you," said he. "Oh, but it's hard to tell."

"Want some whiskey?" I asked, reaching for a decanter that stood handy. He nodded and I gave him good allowance.

"Now," said I, when he'd gulped it down, "let's hear what's turned up."

He looked at me kind of dimly, and I'll be shot if two tears didn't well up in his eyes and run down his cheeks. "I've come to ask you," he said slowly and brokenly, "to ask you — if you won't intercede with Gorgett for me; to ask you if you won't beg him to — to grant me — an interview before to-morrow noon."

"*What!*"

"Will you do it?"

"Certainly. Have you asked for an interview with him yourself?"

He struck the back of his hand across his forehead — struck hard, too.

"Have I tried? I've been following him like a dog since five o'clock this afternoon, beseeching him to give me twenty minutes' talk in private. He *laughed* at me! He isn't a man; he's an iron-hearted devil! Then I went to his house and waited three hours for him. When he came, all he would say was that you were supposed to be running this campaign for me, and I'd better consult with you. Then he turned me out of his house!"

"You seem to have altered a little since this afternoon." I couldn't resist that.

"This afternoon!" he shuddered. "I think that was a thousand years ago!"

"What do you want to see him for?"

"What for? To see if there isn't a little human pity in him for a fellow-being in agony — to end my suspense and know whether or not he means

to ruin me and my happiness and my home forever!''

Farwell didn't seem to be regarding me so
much in the light of a character as usual; still, one
thing puzzled me, and I asked him how he
happened to come to me.

"Because I thought if anyone in the world
could do anything with Gorgett, you'd be the
one," he answered. "Because it seemed to me
he'd listen to you, and because I thought — in
my wild clutching at the remotest hope — that he
meant to make my humiliation more awful by
sending me to you to ask you to go back to him
for me."

"Well, well," I said, " I guess if you want me
to be of any use you'll have to tell me what it's
all about."

"I suppose so," he said, and choked, with a
kind of despairing sound; "I don't see any way
out of it."

"Go ahead," I told him. "I reckon I'm old
enough to keep my counsel. Let it go, Farwell."

"Do you know," he began, with a sharp,

grinding of his teeth, "that dishonourable scoundrel has had me *watched*, ever since there was talk
of me for the fusion candidate? He's had me followed, *shadowed*, till he knows more about me
than I do myself."

I saw right there that I'd never really meas-
ured Gorgett for as tall as he really was. "Have a
cigar?" I asked Knowles, and lit one myself. But
he shook his head and went on:

"You remember my taking you to call on General Buskirk's daughter?"

"Quite well," said I, puffing pretty hard.

"An angel! A white angel! And this beast, this
boodler has the mud in his hands to desecrate her
white garments!"

"Oh," says I.

The angel's knight began to pace the room as
he talked, clinching and unclinching his hands,
while the perspiration got his hair all scraggly on
his forehead. You see Farwell was doing some
suffering and he wasn't used to it.

"When she came home from abroad, a year
ago," he said, "it seemed to me that a light came

into my life. I've got to tell you the whole thing,"
he groaned, "but it's hard! Well, my wife is taken
up with our little boy and housekeeping — I
don't complain of her, mind that — but she
really hasn't entered into my ambitions, my inner
life. She doesn't often read my editorials, and
when she does, she hasn't been serious in her consideration of them and of my purposes. Sometimes she differed openly from me and sometimes greeted my work for truth and light with
indifference! I had learned to bear this, and more;
to save myself pain I had come to shrink from
exposing my real self to her. Then, when this
young girl came, for the first time in my life I
found real sympathy and knew what I thought I
never should know; a heart attuned to my own, a
mind that sought my own ideals, a soul of the
same aspirations — and a perfect faith in what I
was and in what it was my right to attain. She
met me with open hands, and lifted me to my
best self. What, unhappily, I did not find at
home, I found in her — encouragement. I went
to her in every mood, always to be greeted by the

most exquisite perception, always the same delicate receptiveness. She gave me a sister's love!"

I nodded; I knew he thought so.

"Well, when I went into this campaign, what
more natural than that I should seek her ready
sympathy at every turn, than that I should consult with her at each crisis, and, when I became
the fusion candidate, that I should go to her with
the news that I had taken my first great step toward my goal and had achieved thus far in my
struggle for the cause of our hearts — reform?"

"You went up to Buskirk's after the convention?" I asked.

"No; the night before." He took his head in
his hands and groaned, but without pausing in
his march up and down the room. "You remember, it was known by ten o'clock, after the
primaries, that I should receive the nomination.
As soon as I was sure, I went to her; and I found
her in the same state of exaltation and pride that
I was experiencing myself. There was *always* the
answer in her, I tell you, always the response that
such a nature as mine craves. She took both my

hands and looked at me just as a proud sister would. 'I *read* your news,' she said. 'It is in your face!' Wasn't that touching? Then we sat in silence for a while, each understanding the other's joy and triumph in the great blow I had struck for the right. I left very soon, and she came with me to the door. We stood for a moment on the step — and — for the first time, the only time in my life — I received a — a sister's caress."

"Oh," said I. I understood how Gorgett had managed to be so calm that afternoon.

"It was the purest kiss ever given!" Farwell groaned again.

"Who was it saw you?" I asked.

He dropped into a chair and I saw the tears of rage and humiliation welling up again in his eyes.

"We might as well have been standing by the footlights in a theatre!" he burst out, brokenly. "Who saw it? Who *didn't* see it? Gorgett's sleuth-hound, the man he sent to me this afternoon, for one; the policeman on the beat that he'd stopped for a chat in front of the house, for another; a maid in the hall behind us, the policeman's sweetheart *she* is, for another! Oh!" he cried, "the desecration! That one caress, one that I'd thought a sacred secret between us forever — and in plain sight of those three hideous vulgarians, all belonging to my enemy, Gorgett! Ah, the horror of it — what *horror!*"

Farwell wrung his hands and sat, gulping as if he were sick, without speaking for several moments.

"What terms did the man he sent offer from Gorgett?" I asked.

"*No* terms! He said to go ahead and print my story about the closet; it was a matter of perfect indifference to him; that he meant to print this about me in their damnable party-organ to-morrow, in any event, and only warned me so that I should have time to prepare Miss Buskirk. Of course he don't care! *I'll* be ruined, that's all. Oh, the hideous injustice of it, the unreason! Don't you see the frightful irony of it? The best thing in my life, the widest and deepest; my friendship with a good woman becomes a joke and a horror! Don't you see that the personal scandal about me absolutely undermines me and nullifies the political scandal of the closet affair? Gorgett will come in again and the Grand Jury would laugh at any attack on him. I'm ruined for good, for good and all, for good and all!"

"Have you told Miss Buskirk?"

He uttered a kind of a shriek. "*No!* I can't! How could I? What do you think I'm made of? And there's her father — and all her relatives, and mine, and my wife — my wife! If she leaves me — " .

A fit of nausea seemed to overcome him and he struggled with it, shivering. "My God! Do you think I can *face* it? I've come to you for help in the most wretched hour of my life — all darkness, darkness! Just on the eve of triumph to be stricken down — it's so cruel, so devilish! And to think of the horrible comic-weekly misery of it, caught kissing a girl, by a policeman and his sweetheart, the chambermaid! Ugh! The vulgar ridicule — the hideous laughter!" He raised his hands to me, the most grovelling figure of a man I ever saw.

"Oh, for God's sake, help me, help me. . . ."

Well, sir, it was sickening enough, but after he had gone, and I tumbled into bed again, I thought of Gorgett and laughed myself to sleep with admiration.

When Farwell and I got to Gorgett's office, fairly early the next morning, Lafe was sitting there alone, expecting us, of course, as I knew he would be, but in the same characteristic, lazy attitude I'd found him in, the day before; feet up on the desk, hat-brim tilted 'way forward, cigar in the right-hand corner of his mouth, his hands in his pockets, his double-chin mashing down his limp collar. He didn't even turn to look at us as we came in and closed the door.

"Come in, gentlemen, come in," says he, not moving. "I kind of thought you'd be along, about this time."

"Looking for us, were you?" I asked.

"Yes," said he. "Sit down."

We did; Farwell looking pretty pale and red-eyed, and swallowing a good deal.

There was a long, long silence. We just sat and watched Gorgett. *I* didn't want to say anything; and I believe Farwell couldn't. It lasted so long that it began to look as if the little blue haze at the end of Lafe's cigar was all that was going to happen. But by and by he turned his head ever so little, and looked at Knowles.

"Got your story for the *Herald* set up yet?" he asked.

Farwell swallowed some more and just shook his head.

"Haven't begun to work up the case for the Grand Jury yet?"

"No," answered Farwell, in almost a whisper, his head hanging.

"Why," Lafe said, in a tone of quiet surprise; "you haven't given all that up, have you?"

"Yes."

"Well, ain't that strange?" said Lafe. "What's the trouble?"

Knowles didn't answer. In fact, I felt mighty sorry for him.

All at once, Gorgett's manner changed; he

threw away his cigar, the only time I ever saw him do it without lighting another at the end of it. His feet came down to the floor and he wheeled round on Farwell.

"I understand your wife's a mighty nice lady, Mr. Knowles."

Farwell's head sank lower till we couldn't see his face, only his fingers working kind of pitifully.

"I guess you've had rather a bad night?" said Gorgett, inquiringly.

"Oh, my God!" The words came out in a whisper from under Knowles's tilted hat-brim.

"I believe I'd advise you to stick to your wife," Gorgett went on, quietly, "and let politics alone. Somehow I don't believe you're the kind of man for it. I've taken considerable interest in you for some time back, Mr. Knowles, though I don't suppose you've noticed it until lately; and I don't believe you understand the game. You've said some pretty hard things in your paper about me; you've been more or less excitable in your statements; but that's all right. What I don't like altogether, though, is that it seems to me you've

been really tooting your own horn all the time —
calling everybody dishonest and scoundrels, to
shove *yourself* forward. That always ends in sort
of a lonely position. I reckon you feel considerably
lonely, just now? Well, yesterday, I understand
you were talking pretty free about the penitentiary. Now, that ain't just the way to act, according to my notion. It's a bad word. Here we are,
he and I " — he pointed to me — " carrying on our
little fight according to the rules, enjoying it and
blocking each other, gaining a point here and
losing one there, everything perfectly good-
natured, when *you* turn up and begin to talk
about the penitentiary! That ain't quite the thing.
You see words like that are liable to stir up the
passions. It's dangerous. You were trusted, when
they told you the closet story, to regard it as a
confidence — though they didn't go through the
form of pledging you — because your people had
given their word not to betray Genz. But you
couldn't see it and there you went, talking about
the Grand Jury and stripes and so on, stirring up
passions and ugly feelings. And I want to tell you

that the man who can afford to do that has to be mighty immaculate himself. The only way to play politics, whatever you're *for*, is to learn the game first. Then you'll know how far you can go and what your own record will stand. There ain't a man alive whose record will stand too much, Mr. Knowles — and when you get to thinking about that and what your own is, it makes you feel more like treating your fellow-sinners a good deal gentler than you would otherwise. Now *I've* got a wife and two little girls, and my old mother's proud of me (though you wouldn't think it) and they'd hate it a good deal to see me sent over the road for playing the game the best I could as I found it."

He paused for a moment, looking sad and almost embarrassed. "It ain't any great pleasure to me," he said, "to think that the people have let it get to be the game that it is. But I reckon it's good for *you*. I reckon the best thing that ever happened to you is having to come here this morning to ask mercy of a man you looked down on."

Farwell shifted a little in his chair, but he didn't speak, and Gorgett went on:

"I suppose you think it's mighty hard that your private character should be used against you in a political question by a man you call a public corruptionist. But I'm in a position where I can't take any chances against an antagonist that won't play the game my way. I had to find your vulnerable point to defend myself, and, in finding it, I find that there's no need to defend myself any longer, because it makes all your weapons ineffective. I believe the trouble with you, Mr. Knowles, is that you've never realized that politicians are human beings. But we are: we breathe and laugh and like to do right, like other folks. And, like most men, you've thought you were different from other men, and you aren't. So, here you are. I believe you said you'd had a hard night?"

Knowles looked up at last, his lips working for a while before he could speak. "I'll resign now — if you'll — if you'll let me off," he said.

Gorgett shook his head. "I've got the election

in my hand," he answered, "though you fellows don't know it. You've got nothing to offer me, and you couldn't buy me if you had."

At that, Knowles just sank into himself with a little, faint cry, in a kind of heap. There wasn't anything but anguish and despair *to* him. Big tears were sliding down his cheeks.

I didn't say anything. Gorgett sat looking at him for a good while; and then his fat chin began to tremble a little and I saw his eyes shining in the shadow under his old hat-brim.

He got up and went over to Farwell with slow steps and put his hand gently on his shoulder.

"Go on home to your wife," he said, in a low voice that was the saddest I ever heard. "I don't bear you any ill-will in the world. Nobody's going to give you away."

THE ALIENS

PIETRO TOBIGLI, that gay young chestnut vender — he of the radiant smiles — gave forth, in his warm tenor, his own interpretation of "Ach du lieber Augustine," whenever Bertha, rosy waitress in the little German restaurant, showed her face at the door. For a month it had been a courtship; and the merchant sang often:

"*Ahaha, du libra Ogostine,*
Ogostine, Ogostine!
Ahaha, du libra Ogostine,
Nees coma ross."

The acquaintance, begun by the song and Pietro's wonderful laugh, had grown tender. The chestnut vender had a way with him; he looked like the "Neapolitan Fisher Lad" of the chromos, and you could have fancied him of two cen-

turies ago, putting a rose in his hair; even as it
was, he had the ear-rings. But the smile of him
it was that won Bertha, when she came to work
in the little restaurant. It was a smile that put
the world at its ease; it proclaimed the coming of
morning over the meadows, and, taking every
bystander into an April friendship, ran on suddenly into a laugh that was like silver, and like a
strange puppy's claiming you for the lost master.

So it befell that Bertha was fascinated; that,
blushing, she laughed back to him, and was nothing offended when, at his first sight of her, he
rippled out at once into "Ahaha, du libra
Ogostine."

Within two weeks he was closing his business
(no intricate matter) every evening, to walk
home with her, through the September moonlight. Then extraordinary things happened to
the English language.

"I ain'd nefer can like no foreigner!" she
often joked back to a question of his. "Nefer,
nefer! you t'ink I'm takin' up mit a hant-orkan
maan, Mister Toby?"

Whereupon he would carol out the tender taunt, "Ahaha, du libra Ogostine!"

"Yoost a hant-orkan maan!"

"No! *No!* No oragan! I am a greata — greata merchant. Vote a Republican! Polititshian! Tobigli, Chititzen Republican. Naturalasize! March in a parade!"

Never lived native American prouder of his citizenship than this adopted one. Had he not voted at the election? Was he not a member of the great Republican party? He had eagerly joined it, for the reason that he had been a Republican in Italy, and he had drawn with him to the polls his second cousin, Leo Vesschi, and the five other Italians with whom he lived. For this, he had been rewarded by Pixley, his precinct committee-man, who allowed him to carry pink torches in three night processions.

"You keeb oud politigs," said Bertha, earnestly, one evening. "My uncle, Louie Gratz, he iss got a neighbour-lady; her man gone in politigs. After*vorts* he git it! He iss in der bennidenshierry two years. You know why?"

"Democrat!" shouted the chestnut vender triumphantly.

"No, sir! Yoost politigs," replied the unpartisan Bertha. "You keeb oud politigs."

> *"Ahaha, du libra Ogostine,*
> *Ogostine, Ogostine !*
> *Ahaha, du libra Ogostine,*
> *Nees coma ross."*

The song was always a teasing of her and carried all his friendly laughter at her, because of her German ways; but it became softly exultant whenever she betrayed her interest in him.

"Libra Ogostine, she afraid I go penitensh?" he inquired.

"Me!" she jeered with uneasy laughter. "*I* ain'd care! but you — you don' look oud, you git in dod voikhouse!"

He turned upon her, suddenly, a face like a mother's, and touched her hand with a light caress.

"I stay in a workhouse sevena-hunder' year," he said gently, "you come seeta by window some-a-time."

At this Bertha turned away, was silent for a space, leaning on the gate-post in front of her uncle's house, whither they were now come. Finally she answered brokenly: "I ain'd sit by no vinder for yoost a jessnut maan." This was her way of stimulating his ambition.

"Ahaha!" he cried. "You don' know? I'm goin' buy beeg stan'! Candy! Peanut! Banan'! Make some-a-time four dollar a day! 'Tis a greata countra! Bimaby git a store! Ride a buggy! Smoke a cigar! You play piano! Vote a Republican!"

"Toby!"

"'Tis true!"

"Toby," she said tearfully; "Toby, you voik hart, und safe your money?"

"You help?" he whispered.

"I help — *you!*" she cried loudly. Then, with a sudden fit of sobbing, she flung open the gate and ran at the top of her speed into the house.

Halcyon the days for Pietro Tobigli, extravagant the jocularity of this betrothed one. And, as his happiness, so did his prosperity increase; the little chestnut furnace became the smallest adjunct of his affairs; for he leaped (almost at one bound) to the proprietorship of a wooden stand, shaped like the crate of an upright piano and backed up against the brick wall of the restaurant — a mercantile house which was closed at night by putting the lid on. All day long Toby's smile arrested pedestrians, and compelled them to buy of him, making his wares sweeter in the mouth. Bertha dwelt in a perpetual serenade: on warm days, when the restaurant doors were open, she could hear him singing, not always "Ogostine," but festal lilts of Italy, liquid and strangely sweet to her; and at such times, when the actual voice was not in her ears, still she blushed with delight to hear in her heart the thrilling echoes of his barcaroles, and found them humming cheerily upon her own lips.

Toby was to save five hundred dollars before they married, a great sum, but they were patient and both worked very hard. The winter would have fallen bitterly upon an outdoor merchant lacking Toby's confident heart, but on the coldest days, when Bertha looked out, she always found him slapping his hands and trudging up and down in the snow in front of the little box; and, as soon as he caught sight of her — "Aha-ha, du libra Ogostine, Ogostine, Ogostine!"

She saved her own money with German persistence, and on Christmas day her present to her betrothed, in return for a coral pin, was a pair of rubber boots filled with little cakes.

Elysium was the dwelling-place of Pietro Tobigli, though, apparently, he abode in a horrible slum cellar with Leo Vesschi and the five Latti brothers. In this place our purveyor of sweetmeats was the only light. Thither he had carried his songs and his laugh and his furnace when he came from Italy to join Vesschi; and there he remained, partly out of loyalty to his unprosperous comrades, and partly because his share of the expense was only twenty-five cents a week, and every saving was a saving for Ber-

tha. Every evening, on the homeward walk, the
affianced pair passed the hideous stairway that
led down to the cellar, and Bertha, neat soul,
never failed to shudder at it. She did not know
that Pietro lived there, for he feared it might
distress her; nor could she ever persuade him to
tell her where he lived.

Because of this mystery, upon which he mer-
rily insisted, she affected a fear that he would
some day desert her. "You don' tell me where
you lif, I t'ink you goin' ran away of me, Toby.
I vake opp some day; git a ledder dod you gone
back home by 'Talian lady dod's grazy 'bout
you!"

"Ahaha! Libra Ogostine, you believe I can
make a write weet a pen-a-paper? I don' know
that-a *how*. Some-a-time you *see* that gran' palazzo
where I leef. Eesa greata-great sooraprise!"

In the gran' palazzo, it was as much as he
could do to keep clean his own grim little bunk
in the corner. His comrades, sullen, hopeless,
came at evening from ten hours' desperate shov-
elling, and exhibited no ambition for water or

brooms, but sat hunched and silent, or morosely muttering and coughing, in the dark room with its sodden earthen floor, stained walls, and one smoky lamp.

To this uncomfortable chamber repaired, one March evening, Mr. Frank Pixley, Republican precinct committee-man, nor was its dinginess an unharmonious setting for that political brilliant. He was a pock-pitted, damp-looking, soiled little fungus of a man, who had attained to his office because, in the dirtiest precinct of the wickedest ward in the city, he had, through the operation of a befitting ingenuity, forced a recognition of his leadership. From such an office, manned by a Pixley, there leads an upward ramification of wires, invisible to all except manipulators, which extends to higher surfaces. Usually the Pixley is a deep-sea puppet, wholly controlled by the dingily gilded wires that run down to him; but there are times when the Pixley gives forth initial impulses of his own, such as may alter the upper surface; for, in a system of this character, every twitch is felt throughout the whole ramification.

"Hello, boys," the committee-man called out with automatic geniality, as he descended the broken steps. "How are ye? All here? That's good; that's the stuff! Good work!"

Only Toby replied with more than an indifferent grunt; but he ran forward, carrying an empty beer keg which he placed as a seat for the guest.

"Ahaha, Meesa Peeslay! Make a parade? Torchlight? Bandaplay — ta ra, la la la? Firework? Fzzz! Boum! Eh?"

The politician responded to Toby's extravagantly friendly laughter with some mechanical cachinnations which, like an obliging salesman, he turned on and off with no effort. "Not by a dern sight!" he answered. "The campaign ain't begun yet."

"Champagne?" inquired Tobigli politely.

"Campaign, campaign," explained Pixley. "Not much champagne in yours!" he chuckled beneath his breath. "Blame lucky to git Chicago bowl!"

"What is that, that campaign?"

"Why — why, it's the campaign. Workin' up public sentiment; gittin' you boys in line, 'lectioneerin' — fixin' it *right*."

Tobigli shook his head. "Campaign?" he repeated.

"Why — Gee, *you* know! Free beer, cigars, speakin', handshakin', paradin'—"

"Ahaha!" The merchant sprang to his feet with a shout. "Yes! Hoor-r-ra! Vote a Republican! Dam-a Democrat!"

"That's it," replied the committee-man somewhat languidly. "You see, this is a Republican precinct, and it turns the ward —"

"Allaways a Republican!" vociferated Pietro. "That eesa right?"

"Well," said the other, "of course, whichever way you go, you want to follow your precinct committee-man — that's me."

"Yess! Vote a Republican."

Pixley looked about the room, his little red eyes peering out cannily from under his crooked brows at each of the sulky figures in the damp shadows.

"You boys all vote the way Pete says?" he asked.

"Vote same Pietro," answered Vesschi. "Allaways."

"Allaways a Republican," added Pietro sparkingly, with abundant gesture. "'Tis a greata-great countra. Republican here same a Republican at home — eena Etallee. Republican eternall! All good Republican eena thees house! Hoor-r-ra!"

"Well," said Pixley, with a furtiveness half habit, as he rose to go, "of course, you want to keep your eye on your committee-man, and kind of foller along with him, whatever he does. That's me." He placed a dingy bottle on the keg. "I jest dropped in to see how you boys were gittin' along — mighty tidy little place you got here." He changed the stub of his burnt-out cigar to the other side of his mouth, shifting his eyes in the opposite direction, as he continued benevolently: "I thought I'd look in and leave this bottle o' gin fer ye, with my compliments. I'll be around ag'in some evenin', and I reckon before 'lection day comes there may be somep'n doin' — I might

have better fer ye than a bottle. Keep your eye
on me, boys, an' foller the leader. That's the idea.
So long!"

"Vote a Republican!" Pietro shouted after
him gaily.

Pixley turned.

"Jest foller yer leader," he rejoined. "That's
the way to learn politics, boys."

Now as the rough spring wore on into the hap-
pier season, with the days like spiced warm wine,
when people on the street are no longer driven by
the weather but are won by it to loiter; now, indeed, did commerce at Toby's new stand so
mightily thrive that, when summer came, Bertha was troubled as to the safety of Toby's
profits.

"You yoost put your money by der builtun-
loan 'sociation, Toby," she advised gently. "Dey
safe ut fer you."

"T'ree hunder' fifta dolla — *no!*" answered
her betrothed. "I keep in de pock'!" He showed
her where the bills were pinned into his corduroy

waistcoat pocket. "See! Eesa *you!* Onna my heart, libra Ogostine!"

"Toby, uf you ain'd dake ut by der builtun-loan, *blease* put ut in der bink?"

"I keep!" he repeated, shaking his head seriously. "In t'ree-four mont' eesa five-hunder-dolla. Nobody but me eesa tross weet that money."

Nor could Bertha persuade him. It was their happiness he watched over. Who to guard it as he, the dingy, precious parcel of bills? He pictured for himself a swampy forest through which he was laying a pathway to Bertha, and each of the soiled green notes that he pinned in his waistcoat was a strip of firm ground he had made, over which he advanced a few steps nearer her. And Bertha was very happy, even forgetting, for a while, to be afraid of the smallpox, which had thrown out little flags, like auction signs, here and there about the city.

When the full heat of summer came, Pietro laughed at the dog-days; and it was Bertha's to suffer in the hot little restaurant; but she smiled and waved to Pietro, so that he should not know. Also she made him sell iced lemonade and birch beer, which was well for the corduroy waistcoat pocket. Never have you seen a more alluring merchant. One glance toward the stand; you caught that flashing smile, the owner of it a-tip-toe to serve you; and Pietro managed, too, by a light jog to the table on which stood his big, be-dewed, earthen jars, that you became aware of the tinkle of ice and a cold, liquid murmur — what mortal could deny the inward call and pass without stopping to buy?

There fell a night in September when Bertha beheld her lover glorious. She had been warned that he was to officiate in the great opening func-tion of the campaign; and she stood on the corner for an hour before the head of the procession ap-peared. On they came — Pietro's party, three thousand strong; brass bands, fireworks, red fire, tumultuous citizens, political clubs, local potentates in open carriages, policemen, boys, dogs, bicycles — the procession doing all the cheering for itself, the crowds of spectators only feebly responding to this enthusiasm, as is our national custom. At the end of it all marched a plentiful crew of tatterdemalions, a few bleared white men, and the rest negroes. They bore aloft a crazy transparency, exhibiting the legend:

"FRANK PIXLEY'S HARD-MONEY LEAGUE.

WE STAND FOR OUR PRINCIPALS.

WE ARE SOLLID!

NO FOOLING THE PEOPLE GOES!

WE VOTE AS ONE MAN FOR

TAYLOR P. SINGLETON!"

Bertha's eyes had not rested upon Toby where they innocently sought him, in the front ranks, even scanning the carriages, seeking him in all positions which she conceived as highest in honour, and she would have missed him altogether, had not there reached her, out of chaotic clamours, a clear, high, rollicking tenor:

"Ahaha! du libra Ogostine,
Ogostine, Ogostine!
Ahaha! du libra Ogostine,
Nees coma ross!"

Then the eager eyes found their pleasure, for there, in the last line of Pixley's pirates, the very tail of the procession, danced Pietro Tobigli, waving his pink torch at her, proud, happy, triumphant, a true Republican, believing all company equal in the republic, and the rear rank as good as the first.

"Vote a Republican!" he shouted. "Republican — Republican eternall!"

Strangely enough, a like fervid protestation (vociferated in greeting) evoked no reciprocal enthusiasm in the breast of Mr. Pixley, when the committee-man called upon Toby and his friends at their apartment one evening, a fortnight later.

"That's right," he responded languidly. "That's right in gineral, I *should* say. Cert'nly, in *gineral*, I ain't got no quarrel with no man's Republicanism. But this here's kind of a put-tickler case, boys. The election's liable to be mighty close."

"Republican win!" laughed Toby. "Meelyun man eena parade!"

Mr. Pixley's small eyes lowered furtively. He glanced once toward the door, stroked his stubby chin, and answered softly: "Don't you be too sure of that, young feller. Them banks is fightin' each other ag'in!"

"Bank? Fight? W'at eesa that?" inquired the merchant, with an entirely blank mind.

"There's one thing it *ain't*," replied the other, in the same confidential tone. "It ain't no two-by-four campaign. All I got to say to you boys is: 'Foller yer leader'— and you'll wear pearl collar-buttons!"

"Vote a Republican," interjected Leo Vesschi gutturally.

The furtiveness of Mr. Pixley increased.

"Well — mebbe," he responded, very deliberately. "I reckon I better put you boys next, right now's well's any other time. Ain't nothin' ever gained by not bein' open 'n' above-board; that's my motto, and I ack up to it. You kin ast 'em, jest ast the boys, and you'll hear it from each-an-dall: 'Frank Pixley's *square!*' That's what they'll tell ye. Now see here, this is the way it is. I ain't worryin' much about who goes to the legislature, or who's county-commissioners, nor none o' *that. Why* ain't I worryin'? Because it's picayune. It's peanut politics. It ain't where the money is. No, sir, this campaign is on the treasurership. Taylor P. Singleton is runnin' fer treasurer on the Republican ticket, and Gil. Maxim on the Democratic. But that ain't where the fight is." Mr. Pixley spat contemptuously. "Pah! whichever of 'em gits it won't no more'n draw his salary. It's the banks. If Singleton wins out, the Washington National gits the use of the county's money fer the term; if Maxim's elected, Florenheim's bank gits it. Florenheim laid down the cash fer Maxim's nomination, and the Washington National fixed it fer Singleton. And it's big money, don't you git no wrong idea about *that!*"

"Vote a Republican," said Toby politely.

A look of pain appeared upon the brow of the committee-man.

"I reckon I ain't hardly made myself clear," he observed, somewhat plaintively. "Now here, you listen: I reckon it would be kind of resky to trust you boys to scratch the ticket — it's a mixed up business, anyway —"

"Vote a straight!" cried Pietro, nodding his head, cheerfully. "*Yess!* I teach Leo; yess, teach all these"— he waved his hands to indicate the melancholy listeners — "teach them all. Stamp in a circle by that eagle. Vote a Republican!"

"What I was goin' to say," went on the official, exhibiting tokens of impatience and perturbation, "was that if we *should* make any switch this year, I guess you boys would have to switch straight."

"'Tis true!" was the hearty response. "Vote a straight Republican. Republican eternall!"

Pixley wiped his forehead with a dirty handkerchief, and scratched his head. "See here," he said, after a pause, to Toby. "I've got to go down to Collins's saloon, and I'd like to have you come along. Feel like going?"

"Certumalee," answered Toby with alacrity, reaching for his hat.

But no one could have been more surprised than the chestnut vender when, on reaching the vacant street, his companion glancing cautiously about, beckoned him into the darkness of an alley-way, and, noiselessly upsetting a barrel, indicated it as a seat for both.

"Here," said Pixley, "I reckon this is better. Jest two men by theirselves kin fix up a thing like this a lot quicker, and I seen you didn't want to talk too much before *them*. You make your own deal with 'em afterwards, or none at all, jest as you like! They'll do whatever you say, anyway. I sized you up to run *that* bunch, first time I ever laid eyes on the outfit. Now see here, Pete, you listen to me. I reckon I kin turn a little trick here that'll do you some good. You kin bet I see that

the men I pick fer my leaders — like you, Pete
— git their rights! Now here: there's you and the
other six, that's seven; it'll be three dollars in
your pocket if you deliver the goods."

"No! no!" said Pietro in earnest protestation.
"We seven a good Republican. We vote a Republican — same las' time, all a time. Eesa not a
need to pay us to vote a Republican. You save
that a money, Meesa Peaslay."

"You don't understand," groaned Pixley,
with, an inclination to weep over the foreigner's
thick-headedness. "There's a chance fer a big
deal here for all the boys in the precinck. Gil.
Maxim's backers'll pay *big* fer votes enough to
swing it. The best of 'em don't know where
they're at, I tell you. Now here, you see here"—
he took an affectionate grip of Pietro's collar —
"I'm goin' to have a talk with Maxim's manager
to-morrow, I've had one or two a'ready, and I'll
put up the price all round on them people. It's
no more'n right, when you count up what we're
doin' fer them. Look here, you swing them six in
line and march 'em up, and all of ye stamp the

rooster instead of the eagle this time, and help me to show Maxim that Frank Pixley's there with the goods, and I'll hand you a five-dollar bill and a full box o' *cig*ars, see?"

Pietro nodded and smiled through the darkness. "Stamp that eagle!" he answered, "Eesa all *right*, Meesa Peasley. Don't you have afraid. We all seven a good Republican! Stamp that eagle! Hoor-r-ra! Republican *eternall!*"

Pixley was left sitting on the barrel, looking after the light figure of the young man joyously tripping back to the cellar, and turning to wave a hand in farewell from the street.

"Well, I *am* damned!" the politician remarked, with unwitting veracity. "Did the dern Dago bluff me, does he want more, er did he reely didn't un'erstand fer honest?" Then, as he took up his way, crossing the street at the warning of some red and green smallpox lanterns, "I'll git those seven votes, though, *some*way. I'm out fer a record this time, and I'll *git* 'em!"

Bertha went with her fiancé to select the home

that was to be theirs. They found a clean, tidy, furnished room, with a canary bird thrown in, and Toby, in the wild joy of his heart, seized his sweetheart round the waist and tried to force her to dance under the amazed eyes of the landlady.

"You yoost behafed awful!" exclaimed the blushing waitress that evening, with tears of laughter at the remembrance.

She was as happy as her lover, except for two small worries that she had: she feared that her uncle, Louie Gratz, with whom she lived, or one of her few friends, might, when they found she was to marry Toby, allude to him as a "Dago," in which case she had an intuition that he would slap the offender; and she was afraid of the small-pox, which had caused the quarantine of two shanties not far from her uncle's house. The former of her fears she did not mention, but the latter she spoke of frequently, telling Pietro how Gratz was panic-stricken, and talked of moving, and how glad she was that Toby's "gran' pa-lazzo" was in another quarter of the city, as he had led her to believe. Laughing her humours almost away, he told her that the red and green lanterns, threatening murkily down the street, were for only wicked ones, like that Meesa Peaslay, for whom she discovered, Pietro's admiration had diminished. And when she thought of the new home — far across the city from the ugly flags and lanterns — the tiny room with its engraving of the "Rock of Ages" and its canary, she forgot both her troubles entirely; for now, at last, the marvellous fact was assured: the five hundred dollars was pinned into the waistcoat pocket, lying upon Pietro's heart day and night, the precious lump that meant to him Bertha and a home. The good Republican set election-day for the happiest holiday of his life, for that would be his wedding-day.

He left her at her own gate, the evening before that glorious day, and sang his way down the street, feeling that he floated on the airy uplift of his own barcarole beneath sapphire skies, for Bertha had put her arms about him at last.

"Toby," she said, "lieber Toby, I am so all-lofing by you — you are sitch a good maan — I

am so — so — I am yoost all-*lofing* by you!"
And she cried heartily upon his shoulder. "Toby,
uf you ain'd here for me to-morrow by eckseckly
dwelf o'glock, uf you are von minutes late, I'm
goin' yoost fall down deat! Don' you led nothings
happen mit you, Toby."

And she had whispered to him, in love with his
old tender mockery of her, to sing "Libra Ogostine" for her before he said good-night.

Mr. Pixley, again seated upon the barrel
which he had used for his interview with Toby,
beheld the transfigured face of the young man as
the chestnut vender passed the mouth of the
alley, and the committee-man released from his
soul a burdening profanity in the ear of his companion and confidant, a policeman who would
be on duty in Pixley's precinct on the morrow,
and who had now reported for instructions not
necessarily received in a too public rendezvous.

"After I talked to him out here on this very
barrel," said Pixley, his anathema concluded, "I
raised the bid on him; yessir, you kin skin me
fer a dead skunk if I didn't offer him ten dollars

and a box of *cig*ars fer the bunch; and him jest
settin' there laughin' like a plumb fool and tellin' me I didn't need to worry, they'd all vote
Republican fer nothin'! Talked like a parrot:
'Vote a Republican! Republican eternal!' *Republican!* Faugh, he don't know no more why
he's a Republican than a yeller dog'd know! I
went around to-night, when he was out, thought
mebbe I could fix it up with the others. No, *sir!*
Couldn't git nothing out of 'em except some
more parrot-cackle: 'Vote same Petro. All a
good Republican!' It's enough to sicken a
man!"

"Do we need his gang bad?" inquired the
policeman deferentially.

"I need everybody bad! This is a good-sized
job fer me, and I want to do it right. Throwin'
the precinck to Maxim is goin' to do me *some*
wrong with the Republican crowd, even if they
don't git on that it was throwed; and I want to
throw it *good!* I couldn't feel like I'd done right
if I didn't. I've give my word that they'll git a
majority of sixty-eight votes, and that'll be jest

twicet as much in my pocket as a plain majority.
And I want them seven Dagoes! I've give up on
votin' 'em; it can't be done. It'd make a saint
cuss to try to reason with 'em, and it's no good.
They can't be fooled, neither. They know where
the polls is, and they know how to vote — blast
the Australian ballot system! The most that can
be done is to keep 'em away from the polls."

"Can't you git 'em out of town in the morning?"

"D' you reckon I ain't tried that? *No,* sir!
That Dago wouldn't take a pass to *heaven!* Everything else is all right. Doc Morgan's niggers
stays right here and *votes.* I *know* them boys,
and they'll walk up and stamp the rooster all
right, all right. Them other niggers, that Hell-
Valley gang, ain't that kind; and them and
Tooms's crowd's goin' to be took out to Smel-
ter's ice-houses in three express wagons at four
o'clock in the morning. It ain't goin' to cost over
two dollars a head, whiskey and all. Then, Dan
Kelly is fixed, and the Loo boys. Mike, I don't
like to brag, and I ain't around throwin' no bo-

kays at myself as a reg'lar thing, but I want to
say right here, there ain't another man in this
city — no, nor the State neither — that could of
worked his precinck better'n I have this. I tell
you, I'm within five or six votes of the majority
they set for their big money."

"Have you give the Dagoes up altogether?"

"No, by —— !" cried the committee-man
harshly, bringing his dirty fist down on the
other's knee. "Did you ever hear of Frank
Pixley weakenin'? Did you ever see the man that
said Frank Pixley wasn't game?" He rose to his
feet, a ragged and sinister silhouette against the
sputtering electric light at the alley mouth.
"Didn't you ever hear that Frank Pixley had a
barrel of schemes to any other man's bucket
o' wind? What's Frank Pixley's repitation, lemme ast you that? I git what I go after, don't I?
Now look here, you listen to me," he said, low-
ering his voice and shaking a bent forefinger
earnestly in the policeman's face; "I'm goin' to
turn the trick. And I *ought* to do it, too. That
there Pete, he ain't worth the powder to blow

him up — you couldn't learn him no politics if you set up with him night after night fer a year. Didn't I *try? Try?* I dern near bust my head open jest thinkin' up ways to make the flathead *see.* And he wouldn't make no effort, jest set there and parrot out 'Vote a Republican!' He's ongrateful, that's what he is. Well, him and them other Dagoes are goin' to stay at home fer two weeks, beginnin' to-night."

"I'll be dogged if I see how," said the policeman, lifting his helmet to scratch his head.

"I'll show you how. I don't claim no credit fer the idea, I ain't around blowin' my own horn too often, but I'd like fer somebody to jest show me any other man in this city could have thought it out! I'd like to be showed jest one, that's all, jest one! Now, you look here; you see that nigger shanty over there, with the smallpox lanterns outside?"

The policeman shivered slightly. "Yes."

"Look here; they're rebuildin' the pest-house, ain't they?"

"Yes."

"Leavin' smallpox patients in their own holes under quarantine guard till they git a place to put 'em, ain't they?"

"Yes."

"You know how many niggers in that shack?"

"Four, ain't they?"

"Yessir, four of 'em. One died to-night, another's goin' to, another ain't tellin' which way he's goin' yit; and the last one, Joe Cribbins, was the first to take it; and he's almost plumb as good as ever ag'in. He's up and around the house, helpin' nurse the sick ones, and fit fer hard labour. Now look here; that nigger does what I *tell* him and he does it quick — see? Well, he knows what I want him to do to-night. So does Charley Gruder, the guard over there. Charley's fixed; I seen to that; and he knows he ain't goin' to lose no job fer the nigger's gittin' out of the back winder to go make a little sociable call this evening."

"What!" exclaimed the policeman, startled; "Charley ain't goin' to let that nigger out!"

"Ain't he? Oh, you needn't worry, he ain't

goin' *fur!* All he's waiting fer is fer you to give the signal."

"Me!" The man in the helmet drew back.

"Yessir, you! You walk out there and lounge up towards the drug-store and jest look over to Charley and nod twice. Then you stand on the corner and watch and see what you see. When you *see* it, you yell fer Charley and git into the drug store telephone, and call up the health office and git their men up here and into that Dago cellar like hell! The nigger'll be there. They don't know him, and he'll just drop in to try and sell the Dagoes some policy tickets. You understand *me?*"

"Mother Mary in heaven!" The policeman sprang up. "What are you going to do?"

"What am I going to do?" shrilled the other, the light of a monstrous pride in his little eyes. "I'm goin' to quarantine them Dagoes fer fourteen days. They'll learn some politics before I git through with 'em. Maybe they'll know enough United States language to foller their leader next time!"

"By all that's mighty, Pixley," said the policeman, with an admiration that was almost reverence, "you *are* a schemer!"

"Mein Gott!" screeched Bertha's uncle, snapping his teeth fiercely on his pipe-stem, as he flung open the door of the girl's room. "You want to disgraze me mit der whole neighbourhoot, 'lection night? Quid ut! Stob ut! Beoples in der streed stant owidside und litzen to dod grying. You *voult* goin' to marry mit a Dago mens, voult you! Ha, ha! Soife you right! He run away!" The old man laughed unamiably. "Ha, ha! Dago mens foolt dod smard Bertha. Dod's pooty tough. But, bei Gott, you stop dod noise und ect lige a detzent voomans, or you goin' haf droubles mit your uncle Louie Gratz!"

But Bertha, an undistinguishable heap on the floor of the unlit room, only gasped brokenly for breath and wept on.

"Ach, ach, ach, lieber Gott in Himmel!" sobbed Bertha. "Why didn't Toby come for me?

Ach, ach! What iss happened mit Toby? Somedings iss happened — I *know* ut!"

"Ya, ya!" jibed Gratz; "somedings iss heppened, I bet you! Brop'ly he's got anoder vife,
dod's vot heppened! Brop'ly *leffing* ad you mit
anoder voomans! Vot for dit he nefer tolt you
vere he lif? So you voultn't ketch him; dod's der
reason! You're a pooty vun, *you* are! Runnin'
efter a doity Dago mens! Bei Gott! you bedder git
oop und back your glo'es, und stob dod gryin'. I'm
goin' to mofe owid to-morrow; und you kin go
verefer you blease. I ain'd goin' to sday anoder
day in sitch a neighbourhoot. Fife more smallpox lanterns yoost oop der streed. I'm goin' mofe
glean to der oder ent of der city. Und you can
come by me or you can run efter your Dago
mens und his voomans! Dod's why he dittn't
come to marry you, you grazy — ut's a voomans!"

"No, *no*," screamed Bertha, stopping her ears
with her forefingers. "Lies, lies, lies!"

A slatternly negro woman dawdled down the
street the following afternoon, and, encountering

a friend of like description near the cottage which had been tenanted by Louie Gratz and his niece, paused for conversation.

"Howdy, honey," she began, leaning restfully against the gate-post. "How's you ma?"

"She right spry," returned the friend. "How you'self an' you good husban', Miz Mo'ton?"

Mrs. Morton laughed cheerily. "Oh, he enjoyin' de 'leckshum. He 'uz on de picnic yas'day, to Smeltuh's ice-houses; an' 'count er Mist' Maxim's gittin' 'lected, dey gi'n him bottle er whiskey an' two dollahs. He up at de house now, entuhtainin' some ge'lemen frien's wi' de bones, honey."

"Um hum." The other lady sighed reflectively. "I on'y wisht my po' husban' could er live to enjoy de fruits er politics."

"Yas'm," returned Mrs. Morton. "You right. It are a great intrus' in a man's life. Dat what de ornator say in de speech f'm de back er de groce'y wagon, yas'm, a great intrus' in a man's life. Decla'h, I b'lieve Goe'ge think mo' er politics dan he do er me! Well ma'am," she concluded, glancing idly up and down the street and leaning back more comfortably against the gate-post, "I mus' be goin' on my urrant."

"What urrant's dat?" inquired the widow.

"Mighty quare urrant," replied Mrs. Morton. "Mighty quare urrant, honey. You see back yon'eh dat new smallpox flag?"

"Sho."

"Well ma'am, night fo' las', dat Joe Cribbins, dat one-eye nigger what sell de policy tickets, an's done be'n havin' de smallpox, he crope out de back way, when's de gyahd weren't lookin', an', my Lawd, ef dey ain't ketch him down in dat Dago cellar, tryin' sell dem Dagoes policy tickets! Yahah, honey!" Mrs. Morton threw back her head to laugh. "Ain't dat de beatenest nigger, dat one-eyed Joe?"

"What den, Miz Mo'ton?" pursued the listener.

"Den dey quahumteem dem Dagoes; sot a gyahd dah: you kin see him settin' out dah now. Well ma'am, 'cordin' to dat gyahd, one er dem Dagoes like ter go inter fits all day yas'day. Dat man hatter go in an' quiet him down ev'y few minute'. Seem 't he boun' sen' a message an' cain't git no one to ca'y it fer him. De gyahd, he cain't go; he willin' sen' de message, but cain't git nobody come nigh enough de place fer to tell 'em what it is. 'Sides, it 'leckshum-day, an' mos' folks hangin' 'roun' de polls. Well ma'am, dis aft'noon, I so'nter'n by, an' de gyahd holler out an' ask me do I want make a dollah, an' I say I do. I ain't 'fraid no smallpox, done had it two year' ago. So I say I take de message.''

"What is it ?''

"Law, honey, it ain't wrote. Dem Dago folks hain't got no writin' ner readin'. Dey mo' er less like de beasts er de fiel'. Dat message by word er mouf. I goin' tell nuffin 'bout de quahumteem. I'm gotter say: 'Toby sen' word to liebuh Augustine dat she needn' worry. He li'l sick, not much, but de doctah ain' 'low him out fer two weeks; an' 'mejutly at de en' er dat time he come an' git her an' den kin go on home wheres de canary bu'd is.' Honey, you evah hyuh o' sich a foolishness ? But de gyahd, he say de message gotter be ca'yied dass dataways.''

"Lan' name!" ejaculated the widow. "Who dat message to?"

"Hit to a Dutch gal."

"My Lawd!" The widow lifted amazed hands to heaven. "De impidence er dem Dagoes! *Little* mo' an' dey'll be sen'in' messages to you er me! — What her name?"

"Name Bertha Grass," responded Mrs. Morton, "an', nigh as I kin make out, she live in one er dese little w'ite-paint cottages, right 'long yere."

"Yas'm! I knows dat Dutch gal, ole man Grass, de tailor, dass his niece. W'y, dey done move out dis mawn, right f'um dis ve'y house you stan'in in front de gate of. De ole man skeered er de smallpox, an' he mad, too, an' de neighbuhs ask him whuh he gwine, he won't tell; so mad he won't speak to nobody. None on 'em 'round hyuh knows an' dey's considabul cyu'us 'bout it, too. Dey gone off in bofe d'rections — him one way, her 'nother. 'Peah lak dey be'n quollun!"

"Now look at dat!" cried Mrs. Morton dolefully. "Look at dat! Ain't dat de doggonest luck in de wide worl'! De gyahd he say dat Dago willin' pay fifty cents a day fo' me to teck an' bring a message eve'y mawn' tell de quahumteem took off de cellar. Now dat Dutch gal gone an' loss dat money fo' me — movin' 'way whuh nobody cain't fine 'er!'"

"Sho!" laughed the widow. "Ef I'se in you place, Miz Mo'ton, an' you's in mine, dat money sho'lly, sho'lly nevah would be los', indeed hit wouldn't. I dass go in t' de do' an' tu'n right 'roun' back ag'in an' go down to dat gyahd an' say de Dutch gal 'ceive de message wid de bes' er 'bligin' politeness an' sent her kine regyahds to de Dago man an' all inquirin' frien's, an' hope de Dago man soon come an' git 'er. To-morrer de same, nex' day de same —"

"Lawd, ef dat ain't de beatenest!" cried Mrs. Morton delightedly. "Well, honey, I thank you long as I live, 'cause I nevah'd a wuk dat out by myself in de livin' worl', an' I sho does needs de money. I'm goin' do exackly dass de way you say. Dat man he ain' goin' know no diffunce till he git out — an' den, honey," she let loose upon the quiet air a sudden, great salvo of laughter, "dass let him fine Lize Mo'ton!"

Bertha went to live in the tiny room with the canary bird and the engraving of the "Rock of Ages." This was putting lime to the canker, but, somehow, she felt that she could go to no other place. She told the landlady that her young man had not done so well in business as they had expected, and had sought work in another city. He would come back, she said.

She woke from troubled dreams each morning to stifle her sobbing in the pillow. "Ach, Toby, coultn't you sented me yoost one word, you *might* sented me yoost one word, yoost one, to tell me what has happened mit you! Ach, Toby, Toby!"

The canary sang happily; she loved it and tended it, and the gay little prisoner tried to reward her by the most marvellous trilling in his power, but her heart was the sorer for every song.

After a time she went back drearily to the kraut-smelling restaurant, to the work she had thought to leave forever, that day when Toby had not come for her. She went out twenty times every morning, and oftener as it wore on towards evening, to look at his closed stand, always with a choking hope in her heart, always to drag leaden feet back into the restaurant. Several times, her breath failing for shame, she approached Italians in the street, or where there was one to be found at a stand of any sort she stopped and made a purchase, and asked for some word of Toby — without result, always. She knew no other way to seek for him.

One day, as she trudged homeward, two coloured women met on the pavement in front of her, exchanged greetings, and continued for a little way together.

"How you enjoyin' you' money, dese fine days, Miz Mo'ton?" inquired one, with a laugh that attested to the richness of the joke between the two.

"Law, honey," answered the other, "dat good luck di'n' las' ve'y long. Dey done shut off my supplies."

"No!"

"Yas'm, dey sho did. Dat man done tuck de smallpox; all on 'em ketched it, ev'y las' one, off'n dat no 'count Joe Cribbins, an' now dat dey got de new pes'-house finish', dey haul 'em off yon'eh, yas'day. Reckon dat ain' make no diffunce in my urrant runnin'. Dat Dago man, he outer he hade two day fo' dey haul 'em away, an' ain' sen' no mo' messages. So dat spile *my* job! Hit dass my luck. Dey's sho' a voodoo on Lize Mo'ton!"

Bertha, catching but fragments of this conversation, had no realization that it bore in any way upon the mystery of Toby; and she stumbled homeward through the twilight with her tired eyes on the ground.

When she opened the door of the tiny room, the landlady's lean black cat ran out surreptitiously. The bird-cage lay on the floor, upside down, and of its jovial little inhabitant the tokens were a few yellow feathers.

Bertha did not know until a month after, when Leo Vesschi found her at the restaurant and told her, that out in the new pest-house, that other songster and prisoner, the gay little chestnut vender, Pietro Tobigli, had called lamentably upon the name of his God and upon "Libra Ogostine," and now lay still forever, with the corduroy waistcoat and its precious burden tightly clenched to his breast. Even in his delirium they had been unable to coax or force him to part from it for a second.

THE NEED OF MONEY

FAR back in his corner on the Democratic side of the House, Uncle Billy Rollinson sat through the dragging routine of the legislative session, wondering what most of it meant. When anybody spoke to him, in passing, he would answer, in his gentle, timid voice, "Howdy-do, sir." Then his cheeks would grow a little red and he would stroke his long, white beard elaborately, to cover his embarrassment. When a vote was taken, his name was called toward the last of the roll, so that he had ample time, after the leader of his side of the House, young Hurlbut, had voted, to clear his throat several times and say "Aye" or "No" in quite a firm voice. But the instant the word had left his lips he found himself terribly frightened, and stroked his beard a great many times, the while he stared seriously up at the ceiling, partly to avoid meeting anybody's eye, and

partly in the belief that it concealed his agitation
and gave him the air of knowing what he was
about. Usually he did not know, any more than
he knew how he had happened to be sent to the
legislature by his county. But he liked it. He liked
the feeling of being a person to be considered; he
liked to think that he was making the laws of his
State.   He liked the handsome desk and the easy
leather chair; he liked the row of fat, expensive
volumes, the unlimited stationery, and the free
penknives which were furnished him. He enjoyed
the attentions of the coloured men in the cloak-
room, who brushed him ostentatiously and always called him (and the other Representatives)
"Senator," to make up to themselves for the airs
which the janitors of the "Upper House" as-
sumed. Most of these things surprised him; he
had not expected to be treated with such liberal-
ity by the State and never realized that he and his
colleagues were treating themselves to all these
things at the expense of the people, and so, although he bore off as much note-paper as he
could carry, now and then, to send to his son,

Henry, he was horrified and dumbfounded when the bill was proposed appropriating $135,000 for the expenses of the seventy days' session of the legislature.

He was surprised to find that among his "perquisites" were passes (good during the session) on all the railroads that entered the State, and others for use on many inter-urban trolley lines. These, he thought, might be gratifying to Henry, who was fond of travel, and had often been unhappy when his father failed to scrape up enough money to send him to a circus in the next county. It was "very accommodating of the railroads," Uncle Billy thought, to maintain this pleasant custom, because the members' travelling expenses were paid by the State just the same; hence the economical could "draw their mileage" at the Treasurer's office, and add it to their salaries. He heard — only vaguely understanding — many joking references to other ways of adding to salaries.

Most of the members of his party had taken rooms at one of the hotels, whither those who had

sought cheaper apartments repaired in the evening, when the place became a noisy and crowded
club, admission to which was not by card. Most
of the rougher man-to-man lobbying was done
here; and at times it was Babel.

Through the crowds Uncle Billy wandered
shyly, stroking his beard and saying, "Howdy-
do, sir," in his gentle voice, getting out of the way
of people who hurried, and in great trouble of
mind if any one asked him how he intended to
vote upon a bill. When this happened he looked
at the interrogator in the plaintive way which was
his habit, and answered slowly: "I reckon I'll
have to think it over." He was not in Hurlbut's
councils.

There was much bustle all about him, but he
was not part of it. The newspaper reporters remarked the quiet, inoffensive old figure pottering
about aimlessly on the outskirts of the crowd, and
thought Uncle Billy as lonely as a man might well
be, for he seemed less a part of the political ar-
rangement than any member they had ever seen.
He would have looked less lonely and more in

place trudging alone through the furrows of his home fields in a wintry twilight.

And yet, everybody liked the old man, Hurlbut in particular, if Uncle Billy had known it; for Hurlbut watched the votes very closely and was often struck by the soundness of Representative Rollinson's intelligence in voting.

In return, Uncle Billy liked Hurlbut better than any other man he had ever known — except Henry, of course. On the first day of the session, when the young leader had been pointed out to him, Uncle Billy's humble soul was prostrate with admiration, and when Hurlbut led the first attack on the monopolistic tendencies of the Republican party, Representative Rollinson, chuckling in his beard at the handsome youth's audacity, himself dared so greatly as to clap his hands aloud. Hurlbut, on the floor, was always a storm centre: tall, dramatic, bold, the members put down their newspapers whenever his strong voice was heard demanding recognition, and his "Mr. Speaker!" was like the first rumble of thunder. The tempest nearly always followed, and there were times

when it threatened to become more than vocal;
when, all order lost, nine-tenths of the men on the
other side of the House were on their feet shouting jeers and denunciations, and the orator faced
them, out-thundering them all, with his own co-
horts, flushed and cheering, gathered round him.
Then, indeed, Uncle Billy would have thought
him a god, if he had known what a god was.

Sometimes Uncle Billy saw him in the hotel
lobby, but he seemed always to be making for the
elevator in a hurry, with half-a-dozen people trying to detain him, or descending momentarily
from the stairway for a quick, sharp talk with one
or two members, their heads close together, after
which Hurlbut would dart upward again.

Sometimes the old man sat down at one of the
writing tables, in a corner of the lobby, and, an-
nexing a sheet of the hotel note-paper, "wrote
home" to Henry. He sat with his head bent far
over, the broad brim of his felt hat now and then
touching the hand with which he kept the paper
from sliding; and he pressed diligently upon his
pen, usually breaking it before the letter was fin-

ished. He looked so like a man intent upon concealment that the reporters were wont to say: "There's Uncle Billy humped up over his guilty secret again."

The secret usually took this form:

" Dear Son Henry:

" I would be glad if you was here. There is big doings. Hurlbut give it to them to-day. He don't give the Republicans no rest. he lights into them like sixty you would like to see him. They are plenty nice fellows in the Republicans too but they lay mighty low when Hurlbut gets after them. He was just in the office but went out. He always has a segar in his mouth but not lit. I expect hes quit. I send you enclosed last week's salary all but $11.80 which I had to use as living is pretty high in our capital city of the state. If you would like some of this hotel writing paper better than the kind I sent you of the General Assembly I can send you some the boys say it is free. I think it is all right you sold the calf but Wilkes didn't give you good price. Hurlbut come in while I was writing then. You bet he can always count on Wm. Rollinson's vote.

" Well I must draw to a close,   Yours truly

" Your father."

"Wm. Rollinson" was not aware that he was known to his colleagues and the lobby and the Press as "Uncle Billy" until informed thereof by a public print. He stood, one night, on the edge of a laughing group, when a reporter turned to him and said:

"The *Constellation* would like to know Representative Rollinson's opinion of the scandalous story that has just been told."

The old man, who had not in the least understood the story, summoned all his faculties, and, after long deliberation, bent his plaintive eyes upon the youth and replied:

"Well, sir, it's a-stonishing, a-stonishing!"

"Think it's pretty bad, do you?"

Some of the crowd turned to listen, and the old fellow, hopelessly puzzled, stroked his beard with a trembling hand, and then, muttering, "Well, young man, I expect you better excuse me," hurried away and left the place. The next morning he found the following item tacked to the tail of the "Legislative Gossip" column of the *Constellation:*

"UNCLE BILLY ROLLINSON HORRIFIED

"Yesterday a curious and amusing story was current among the solons at the Nagmore Hotel. It seems that the wife of a country member of the last legislature had been spending the day at the hotel and the wife of a present member from the country complained to her of the greatly increased expenditure appertaining to the cost of living in the Capital City. 'Indeed,' replied the wife of the former member, 'that is curious. But I suppose my husband is much more economical than yours, for he brought home $1.500, that he'd saved out of his salary.' As the salary is only $456, and the gentleman in question did not play poker, much hilarity was indulged in, and there were conjectures that the economy referred to concerned his vote upon a certain bill before the last session, anent which the lobby pushing it were far from economical. Uncle Billy Rollinson, the Gentleman from Wixinockee, heard the story, as it passed from mouth to mouth, but he had no laughter to greet it. Uncle Billy, as every one who comes in contact with him knows, is as honest as the day is long, and the story grieved and shocked him. He expressed the utmost horror and consternation, and requested to be excused from speaking further upon a subject so repugnant to his feelings. If there were more men of this stamp in politics, who find corruption revolting instead of amusing, our legislatures would enjoy a better fame."

Uncle Billy had always been agitated by the sight of his name in print. Even in the Wixinockee County *Clarion*, it dumbfounded him and gave him a strange feeling that it must mean somebody else, but this sudden blaze of metropolitan fame made him almost giddy. He folded the paper quickly and placed it under his coat, feeling vaguely that it would not do to be seen reading it. He murmured feeble answers during the day, when some of his colleagues referred to it; but when he reached his own little room that evening, he spread it out under his oil-smelling lamp and read it again. Perhaps he read it twenty times over before the supper bell rang. Perhaps the fact that he was still intent upon it accounted for his not hearing the bell, so that his landlady had to call him.

What he liked was the phrase: "Honest as the day is long." He did not go to the hotel that night.

He went back to his room and read the *Constellation*. He liked the *Constellation*. Newspapers were
very kind, he thought. Now and then, he would
pick up his pile of legislative bills and try to spell
through the ponderous sentences, but he always
gave it up and went back to the *Constellation*. He
wondered if Hurlbut had read it. Hurlbut had.
The leader had even told the author of the item
that he was glad somebody could appreciate the
kind of a man Uncle Billy was, and his value to
the body politic.

"Honest as the day is long," Uncle Billy repeated to himself, in the little room, nodding his
head gravely. Then he thought for a long while
about the member who had, according to the
story, gone home with $1,500. He sat up, that
evening, until almost ten o'clock. Even after he
had gone to bed, he lay awake with his eyes wide
open in the darkness, thinking of the colossal
sum. If anybody should come to *him* and offer
him all that money to vote a certain way upon a
bill, he believed he would not take it, for that
would be bribery; though Henry would be

glad to have the money. Henry always needed
money; sometimes the need was imperative —
once, indeed, so imperative that the small, un-
fertile farm had been mortgaged beyond its value,
otherwise very serious things must have happened to Henry. Uncle Billy wondered how offers
of money to members were refused without hurt-
ing the intending donor's feelings. And what a
great deal could be done with $1,500, if a member
could get it and still be as honest as the day is
long!

About the second month of the session, the floor
of the House began steadily to grow more and
more tumultuous. To an unpolitical onlooker,
leaning over the gallery rail, it was often an in-
comprehensible Bedlam, or perhaps one might
have been reminded of an ant-heap by the hurry-
and-scurry and life-and-death haste in a hundred
directions at once, quite without any distinguish-
able purpose. Twenty men might be rampaging
up and down the aisles, all shouting, some of
them furiously, others with a determination that
was deadly, all with arms waving at the Speaker.

some of the hands clenched, some of them fluttering documents, while pages ran everywhere in
mad haste, stumbling and falling in the aisles. In
the midst of this, other members, seated, wrote
studiously; others mildly read newspapers; others
lounged, half-standing against their desks, un-
lighted cigars in their mouths, laughing; all the
while the patient Speaker tapped with his gavel on
a small square of marble. Suddenly perfect calm
would come and the voice of the reading-clerk
drone for half an hour or more, like a single bee
in a country garden on Sunday morning.

Of all this Uncle Billy was as much a layman
spectator as any tramp who crept into the gallery
for a few hours out of the cold. The hurry and
seethe of the racing sea touched him not at all,
except to bewilderment, while he was carried with
it, unknowing, toward the breakers. The shout of
those breakers was already in the ears of many,
for the crisis of the session was coming. This was
the fight that was to be made on Hurlbut's
"Railroad Bill," which was, indeed, but in another sense, known as the "Breaker."

Uncle Billy had heard of the "Breaker." He couldn't have helped that. He had heard a dozen say: "Then's when it's going to be warm times, when that 'Breaker' comes up!" or, "Look out for that 'Breaker.' We're going to have big trouble." He knew, too, that Hurlbut was interested in the "Breaker," but upon which side he was for a long time ignorant.

Hurlbut always nodded to the old man, now, as he came down the aisle to his own desk. He had begun that, the day after the *Constellation* item. Uncle Billy never failed to be in his seat early in the morning, waiting for the nod. He answered it with his usual "Howdy-do, sir," then stroked his beard and gazed profoundly at the row of fat volumes in front of him, swallowing painfully once or twice.

This was all that really happened for Uncle Billy during the turmoil and scramble that went on about him all the day long. He had not been forced to discover a way to meet an offer of $1,500, without hurting the putative giver's feelings. No lobbyist had the faintest idea of "approaching" the old man in that way. The members and the hordes of camp-followers and all the lobby had settled into a belief that Representative Rollinson was a sea-green Incorruptible, that of all honest members he was the most honest. He had become typical of honesty: sayings were current — "You might as well try to bribe Uncle Billy Rollinson!" "As honest as old Uncle Billy Rollinson." Hurlbut often used such phrases in private.

The "Breaker" was Hurlbut's own bill; he had planned it and written it, though it came over to the House from the Senate under a Senator's name. It was one of those "anti-monopolistic" measures which Democrats put their whole hearts into, sometimes, and believe in and fight for magnificently; an idea conceived in honesty and for a beneficent purpose, in the belief that a legislature by the wave of a hand can conjure the millennium to appear; and born out of an utter misconception of man and railroads. The bill needs no farther description than this: if it passed and became an enforced law, the dividends of every railroad entering the State would be reduced by two-fifths. There is one thing that will fight harder than a Democrat — that is a railroad.

The "Breaker" had been kept very dark until Hurlbut felt that he was ready; then it was swept through the Senate before the railroad lobby, previously lulled into unsuspicion, could collect itself and block it. This was as Hurlbut had planned: that the fight should be in his own House. It was the bill of his heart and he set his reputation upon it. He needed fifty-one votes to pass it, and he had them, and one to spare; for he took his followers, who formed the majority, into caucus upon it. It was in the caucus Uncle Billy learned that Hurlbut was "for" the bill. He watched the leader with humble, wavering eyes, thinking how strong and clear his voice was, and wondering if he never lit the cigar he always carried in his hand, or if he ever got into trouble, like Henry, being a young man. If he did, Uncle Billy would have liked the chance to help him out.

He had plenty of such chances with Henry; indeed, the opportunity may be said to have become unintermittent, and Uncle Billy was never free from a dim fear of the day when his son would get in so deeply that he could not get him out. Verily, the day seemed near at hand: Henry's letters were growing desperate and the old man walked the floor of his little room at night, more and more hopeless. Once or twice, even as he sat at his desk in the House, his eyes became so watery that he forced himself into long spells of coughing, to account for it, in case any one might be noticing him.

The caucus was uneventful and quiet, for it had all been talked over, and was no more than a matter of form.

The Republicans did not caucus upon the bill (they had reasons), but they were solidly against it. Naturally it follows that the assault of the railroad lobby had to be made upon the virtue of the Democrats *as* Democrats. That is, whether a member upon the majority side cared about the bill for its own sake or not, right or wrong, he felt it his duty as a Democrat to vote for it. If he had a conscience higher than a political conscience, and believed the bill was bad, his duty was to "bolt the caucus"; but all of the Democratic side believed in the righteousness of the bill, except two. One had already been bought and the other was Uncle Billy, who knew nothing about it, except that Hurlbut was "for" it and it seemed to be making a "big stir."

The man who had been bought sat not far from Uncle Billy. He was a furtive, untidy slouch of a man, formerly a Republican; he had a great capacity for "handling the coloured vote" and his name was Pixley. Hurlbut mistrusted him; the young man had that instinct, which good leaders need, for feeling the weak places in his following; and he had the leader's way, too, of ever bracing up the weakness and fortifying it; so he stopped, four or five times a day, at Pixley's desk, urging the necessity of standing fast for the "Breaker," and expressing convictions as to the political future of a Democrat who should fail to vote for it; to which Pixley assented in his husky, tough-ward voice.

All day long now, Hurlbut and his lieutenants, disregarding the routine of bills, went up and down the lines, fending off the lobbyists and such Republicans as were working openly for the bill. They encouraged and threatened and never let themselves be too confident of their seeming strength. Some of those who were known, or guessed, to be of the "weaker brethren" were not left to themselves for half an hour at a time, from their breakfasts until they went to bed. There was always at elbow the "*Hold fast!*" whisper of Hurlbut and his lieutenants. None of them ever thought of speaking to Uncle Billy.

Hurlbut's "work was cut out for him," as they said. What work it is to keep every one of fifty men honest under great temptation for three weeks (which time it took for the hampered and filibustered bill to come up for its passage or defeat), is known to those who have tried to do it. The railroads were outraged and incensed by the measure; they sincerely believed it to be monstrous and thievish. "Let the legislature try to confiscate two-fifths of the lawyers', or the bakers', or the ironmoulders', just earnings," said they, "and see what will happen!"

When such a bill as this comes to the floor for the third time the fight is already over, oratory is futile; and Cicero could not budge a vote. The railroads were forced to fight as best they could; this was the old way that they have learned is most effective in such a case. Votes could not be had to "oblige a friend" on the "Breaker" bill; nor could they be procured by arguments to prove the bill unjust. In brief: the railroad lobby had no need to buy Republican votes (with the exception of the one or two who charged out of habit whenever legislation concerned corporations), for the Republicans were against the bill, but they did mortally need to buy two Democratic votes, and were willing to pay handsomely for them. Nevertheless, Mr. Pixley's price was not exorbitant, considering the situation; nor need he have congratulated himself so heartily as he did (in moments of retirement from public life) upon his prospective $2,000 (when the goods should be delivered) since his vote was assisting the railroads to save many million dollars a year.

Of course the lobby attacked the bill noisily; there were big guns going all day long; but those in charge knew perfectly well that the noise accomplished nothing in itself. It was used to cover the whispering. Still, Hurlbut held his line firm and the bill passed its second reading with fifty-two votes, Mr. Pixley being directed by his owners to vote for it on that occasion.

As time went on, the lobby began to grow desperate; even Pixley had been consulted upon his opinion by Barrett, the young lawyer through whom negotiations in his case had been conducted. Pixley suggested the name of Rollinson and Barrett dismissed this counsel with as much disgust for Pixley's stupidity as he had for the man's person. (One likes a *dog* when he buys him.)

"But why not?" Pixley had whined as he reached the door. "Uncle Billy ain't so much! You listen to me. He wouldn't take it out-an'-out — I don't say as he would. But you needn't work that way. Everybody thinks it's no use to tackle him — but nobody never *tried!* What's he *done* to make you scared of him? *Nothing!* Jest set there and *looked!*"

After he had gone the fellow's words came back to Barrett: "Nobody never tried!" And then, to satisfy his conscience that he was leaving no stone unturned, yet laughing at the uselessness of it, he wrote a letter to a confidant of his, formerly a colleague in the lobby, who lived in the county-seat near which Uncle Billy's mortgaged acres lay. The answer came the night after the second vote on the "Breaker."

"Dear Barrett:

"I agree with your grafter. I don't believe Rollinson would be hard to approach if it were done with tact — of course you don't want to tackle him the way you would a swine like Pixley. A good many people around here always thought the old man simple-minded. He was given the nomination almost in joke — nobody else wanted it, because they all thought the Republicans had a sure thing of it; but Rollinson slid in on the general Democratic landslide in this district. He's got one son, a worthless pup, Henry, a sort of yokel Don Juan, always half drunk when his father has any money to give him, and just smart enough to keep the old man mesmerized. Lately Henry's been in a mighty serious peck of trouble. Last fall he got married to a girl here in town. Three weeks ago a family named Johnson, the most shiftless in the county, the real low-down white trash sort, living on a truck patch out Rollinson's way, heard that Henry was on a toot in town, spending money freely, and they went after him. A client of mine rents their ground to them and told me all about it. It seems they claim that one of the daughters in the Johnson family was Henry's common-law wife before he married the other girl, and it's more than likely they can prove it. They are hollering for $600, and if Henry doesn't raise it mighty quick they swear they'll get him sent over the road for bigamy. I think the old man would sell his soul to keep his boy out of the penitentiary and he's at his wits' ends; he hasn't anything to raise the money on and he's up against it. He'll do any thing on earth for Henry. Hope this'll be of some service to you, and if there's anything more I can do about it you better call me up on the long distance.

" Yours faithfully,
" J. P. Watson.

" P. S. — You might mention to our old boss that I don't want anything if services are needed; but a pass for self and family to New York and return would come in handy."

Barrett telegraphed an answer at once: "If it goes you can have annual for yourself and family. Will call you up at two sharp to-morrow."

It was late the following night when the lobbyist concluded his interview with Representative Rollinson, in the latter's little room, half lighted by the oil-smelling lamp.

"I knew you would understand, Mr. Rollinson," said Barrett as he rose to go. His eyes danced and his jaws set with the thought that had been jubilant within him for the last half-hour: "We've got 'em! We've got 'em! We've got 'em!" The railroads had defended their own again.

"Of course," he went on, "we wouldn't have dreamed of coming to you and asking you to vote against this outrageous bill if we thought for a minute that you had any real belief in it or considered it a good bill. But you say, yourself, your only feeling about it was to oblige Mr. Hurlbut, and you admit, too, that you've voted his way on every other bill of the session. Surely, as I've

already said so many times, you don't think he'd
be so unreasonable as to be angry with you for
differing with him on the merits of only one! No,
no, Hurlbut's a very sensible fellow about such
matters. You don't need to worry about *that!*
After all I've said, surely you won't give it another
thought, will you?"

Uncle Billy sat in the shadow, bent far over,
slowly twisting his thin, corded hands, the fingers
tightly interlocked. It was a long time before he
spoke, and his interlocutor had to urge him again
before he answered, in his gentle, quavering
voice.

"No, I reckon not, if you say so."

"Certainly not," said Barrett briskly. "Why
of course, we'd never have thought of making you
a money offer to vote either for or against your
principles. Not much! We don't do business
that way! We simply want to do something for
you. We've wanted to, all during the session,
but the opportunity hadn't offered until I happened to hear your son was in trouble."

Out of the shadow came a long, tremulous

sigh. There was a moment's pause; then Uncle
Billy's head sank slowly lower and rested on his
hands.

"You see," the other continued cheerfully,
"we make no conditions, none in the world. We
feel friendly to you and want to oblige you, but of
course we do think you ought to show a little
good-will towards *us*. I believe it's all understood: to-morrow night Mr. Watson will drive
out in his buggy to this Johnson place, and he's
empowered by us to settle the whole business and
obtain a written statement from the family that
they have no claim on your son. How he will
settle it is neither your affair nor mine; nor
whether it costs money or not. But he *will*
settle it. We do that out of good-will to you, as
long as we feel as friendly to you as we do now,
and all we ask is that you show your good-will to
us."

It was plain, even to Uncle Billy, that if he voted
against Mr. Barrett's friends in the afternoon
those friends might not feel so much good-will
toward him in the evening as they did now; and

Mr. Watson might not go to the trouble of hitching up his buggy to drive out to the Johnsons'.

"You see, it's all out of friendship," said Barrett, his hand on the door knob. "And we can count on your's to-morrow, can't we — absolutely?"

The grey head sank a little lower, and then after a moment the quavering voice answered:

"Yes, sir — I'll be friendly."

Before morning, Hurlbut lost another vote. One of his best men left on a night train for the bedside of his dying wife. This meant that the "Breaker" needed every one of the fifty-one remaining Democratic votes in order to pass. Hurlbut more than distrusted Pixley, yet he felt sure of the other fifty, and if, upon the reading of the bill, Pixley proved false, the bill would not be lost, since there would be a majority of votes in its favour, though not the constitutional majority of fifty-one required for its passage, and it could be brought up again and carried when the absent man returned. Thus, on the chance that Pixley had withstood tampering, Hurlbut made no effort to prevent the bill from coming to the floor in its regular order in the afternoon, feeling that it could not possibly be killed by a majority against it, for he trusted his fifty, now, as strongly as he distrusted Pixley.

And so the roll-call on the "Breaker" began, rather quietly, though there was no man's face in the hall that was not set to show the tensity of high-strung nerves. The great crowd that had gathered and choked the galleries and the floor beyond the bar, and the Senators who had left their own chamber to watch the bill in the House, all began to feel disappointed; for nothing happened until Pixley's name was called.

Pixley voted "No!"

Uncle Billy, sitting far down in his leather chair on the small of his back, heard the outburst of shouting that followed; but he could not see Pixley, for the traitor was instantly surrounded by a ring of men, and all that was visible from where he sat was their backs and upraised, gesticulating hands. Uncle Billy began to tremble violently; he had not calculated on this; but surely such things would not happen to *him!*

The Speaker's gavel clicked through the up-roar and the roll-call proceeded.

The clerk reached the name of Rollinson. Uncle Billy swallowed, threw a pale look about him and wrapped his damp hands in the skirts of his shiny old coat, as if to warm them. For a moment he could not answer. People turned to look at him.

"Rollinson!" shouted the clerk again.

"No," said Uncle Billy.

Immediately he saw above him and all about him a blur of men's faces and figures risen to their feet, he heard a hundred voices say breathlessly: "*What!*" and one that said: "My God, that kills the bill!"

Then a horrible and incredible storm burst upon him, and he who had sat all the session shrinking unnoticed in his quiet, back seat, un-nerved when a colleague asked the simplest ques-tion, found himself the centre and point of at-tack in the wildest mêlée that legislature ever saw.

A dozen men, red, frantic, with upraised arms, came at him, Hurlbut the first of them. But the lobby was there, too; for it was not part of its calculations that the old man should be frightened into changing his vote.

There need have been no fear of that. Uncle Billy was beyond the power of speech. The lobby's agents swarmed on the floor, and, with half-a-dozen hysterically laughing Republicans, met the onset of Hurlbut and his men. It became a riot immediately. Sane men were swept up in it to be as mad as the rest, while the galleries screamed and shouted. All round the old man the fury was greatest; his head sank over his desk and rested on his hands as it had the night before; for he dared not lift it to see the avalanche he had loosed upon himself. He would have liked to stop his ears to shut out the egregious clamour of cursing and yelling that beset him, as his bent head kept the glazed eyes from seeing the impossible vision of the attack that strove to reach him. He remembered awful dreams that were like this; and now, as then, he shuddered in a cold sweat, being as one who would draw the covers over his head to shelter him from horrors in great darkness. As Uncle Billy felt, so might a naked soul feel at the judgment day, tossed alone into the pit with all the myriads of eyes in the universe fastened on its sins.

He was pressed and jostled by his defenders; once a man's shoulders were bent back down over his own and he was crushed against the desk until his ribs ached; voices thundered and wailed at him, threatening, imploring, cursing, cajoling, raving.

Smaller groups were struggling and shouting in every part of the room, the distracted sergeants-at-arms roaring and wrestling with the rest. On the high dais the Speaker, white but imperturbable, having broken his gavel, beat steadily with the handle of an umbrella upon the square of marble on his desk. Fifteen or twenty members, raging dementedly, were beneath him, about the clerk's desk and on the steps leading up to his chair, each howling hoarsely:

"A point of *order!* A point of *or-der!*"

When the semblance of order came at last, the
roll was finished, "reconsidered," the "Breaker"
was beaten, 50 to 49, was dead; and Uncle Billy
Rollinson was creeping down the outer steps of
the Statehouse in the cold February slush and
rain.

He was glad to be out of the nightmare, though
it seemed still upon him, the horrible clamours,
all gonging and blaring at *him;* the red, madden-
ed faces, the clenched fists, the open mouths, all
raging at *him* — all the ruck and uproar swam
about the dazed old man as he made his slow, un-
seeing way through the wet streets.

He was too late for dinner at his dingy boarding house, having wandered far, and he found
himself in his room without knowing very well
how he had come there, indeed, scarcely more
than half-conscious that he *was* there. He sat, for
a long time, in the dark. After a while he me-
chanically lit the lamp, sat again to stare at it,
then, finding his eyes watering, he turned from it
with an incoherent whimper, as if it had been a
person from whom he would conceal the fact that

he was weeping. He leaned his arm against the window sill and dried his eyes on the shiny sleeve.

An hour later, there came a hard, imperative knock on the door. Uncle Billy raised his head and said gently:

"Come in."

He rose to his feet uncertain, aghast, when he saw who his visitor was. It was Hurlbut.

The young man confronted him darkly, for a moment, in silence. He was dripping with rain; his hat, unremoved, shaded lank black locks over a white face; his nostrils were wide with wrath; the "dry cigar" wagged between gritting teeth.

"Will ye take a chair?" faltered Uncle Billy.

The room rang to the loud answer of the other: "I'd see you in Hell before I'd sit in a chair of yours!"

He raised an arm, straight as a rod, to point at the old man. "Rollinson," he said, "I've come here to tell you what I think of you! I've never done that in my life before, because I never thought any man worth it. I do it because I need the luxury of it — because I'm sick of myself not

to have had gumption enough to see what you
were all the time and have you watched!"

Uncle Billy was stung to a moment's life.
"Look here," he quavered, "you hadn't ought to
talk that way to me. There ain't a cent of money
passed my fingers — "

Hurlbut's bitter laugh cut him short. "*No?*
Don't you suppose *I know* how it was done? Do
you suppose there's a man in the whole Assembly
doesn't know how you were sold? I had it by the
long distance an hour ago, from your own home.
Do you suppose *we* have no friends there, or that
it was hard to find out about the whole dirty business? Your son's not going to stand trial for big-
amy; that was the price you charged for killing the
bill. You and Pixley are the only men whom they
could buy with all their millions! Oh, I know a
dozen men who could be bought on other issues,
but not on *this!* You and Pixley stand alone. Well,
you've broken the caucus and you've betrayed the
Democratic party. I've come to tell you that the
party doesn't want you any more. You are out of
it, do you hear? We don't want even to use you!"

The old man had sunk back into his chair, stricken white, his hands fluttering helplessly. "I didn't go to hurt your feelings, Mr. Hurlbut," he said. "I never knowed how it would be, but I don't think you ought to say I done anything dishonest. I just felt kind of friendly to the rail-roads — "

The leader's laugh cut him off again. "Friend-ly! Yes, that's what you were! Well, you can go back to your friends; you'll need them! — Mother in Heaven! How you fooled us! We thought you were the straightest man and the staunchest Democrat — "

"I b'en a Democrat all my life, Mr. Hurlbut. I voted fer — "

"Well, you're a Democrat no longer. You're done for, do you understand? And we're done with you!"

"You mean," the old man's voice shook al-most beyond control; "you mean you're tryin' to read me out of the party?"

"Trying to!" Hurlbut turned to the door. "You're out! It's done. You can thank God that your 'friends' did their work so well that we can't prove what we know. On my soul, you dog, if we could I believe some of the boys would send you over the road."

An hour after he had gone, Uncle Billy roused himself from his stupor, and the astonished landlady heard his shuffling step on the stair. She followed him softly and curiously to the front door, and watched him. He was bare-headed but had not far to go. The night-flare of the cheap, all-night saloon across the sodden street silhouetted the stooping figure for a moment and then the swinging doors shut the old man from her view. She returned to her parlour and sat waiting for his return until she fell asleep in her chair. She awoke at two o'clock, went to his room, and was aghast to find it still vacant.

"The Lord have mercy on us all!" she cried aloud. "To think that old rascal'd go out on a spree! He'd better of stayed in the country where he belonged."

It was the next morning that the House received a shock which loosed another riot, but one of a kind different from that which greeted Representative Rollinson's vote on the "Breaker." The reading-clerk had sung his way through an inconsequent bill; most of the members were buried in newspapers, gossiping, idling, or smoking in the lobbies, when a loud, cracked voice was heard shrilly demanding recognition.

"Mr. Speaker!" Every one turned with a start. There was Uncle Billy, on his feet, violently waving his hands at the Speaker. "Mr. Speaker, Mr. Speaker, Mr. Speaker!" His dress was disordered and muddy; his eyes shone with a fierce, absurd, liquorish light; and with each syllable that he uttered his beard wagged to an unspeakable effect of comedy. He offered the most grotesque spectacle ever seen in that hall — a notable distinction.

For a moment the House sat in paralytic astonishment. Then came an awed whisper from a Republican: "Has the old fool really found his voice?"

"No, he's drunk," said a neighbour. "I guess he can afford it, after his vote yesterday!"

"Mister Speaker! *Mister* Speaker!"

The cracked voice startled the lobbies. The hangers-on, the typewriters, the janitors, the smoking members came pouring into the chamber and stood, transfixed and open-mouthed.

"*Mister Speaker!*"

Then the place rocked with the gust of laughter and ironical cheering that swept over the Assembly. Members climbed upon their chairs and on desks, waving handkerchiefs, sheets of foolscap, and waste-baskets. "Hear 'im! *He-ear* 'im!" rang the derisive cry.

The Speaker yielded in the same spirit and said:

"The Gentleman from Wixinockee."

A semi-quiet followed and the cracked voice rose defiantly:

"That's who I am! I'm the Gentleman from Wixinockee an' I stan' here to defen' the principles of the Democratic party!"

The Democrats responded with violent hootings, supplemented by cheers of approval from the Republicans. The high voice out-shrieked

them all: "Once a Democrat, always a Democrat! I voted Dem'cratic tick't forty year, born a
Democrat an' die a Democrat. Fellow sizzens, I
want to say to you right here an' now that principles of Dem'cratic party saved this country a
hun'erd times from Republican mal-'diminis-
tration an' degerdation! Lemme tell you this:
you kin take my life away but you can't say I
don' stan' by Dem'cratic party, mos' glorious
party of Douglas an' Tilden, Hen'ricks, Henry
Clay, an' George Washin'ton. I say to you they
hain't no other party an' I'm member of it
till death an' Hell an' f'rever after, so help
me *God!*"

He smote the desk beside him with the back
of his hand, using all his strength, skinning his
knuckles so that the blood dripped from them, unnoticed. He waved both arms continually, bending his body almost double and straightening up
again, in crucial efforts for emphasis. All the old
jingo platitudes that he had learned from campaign speakers throughout his life, the nonsense
and brag and blat, the cheap phrases, all the

empty balderdash of the platform, rushed to his incoherent lips.

The lord of misrule reigned at the end of each sentence, as the members sprang again upon the chairs and desks, roaring, waving, purple with laughter. The Speaker leaned back exhausted in his chair and let the gavel rest. Spectators, pages, galleries whooped and howled with the members. Finally the climax came.

"I want to say to you just this *here*," shrilled the cracked voice, "an' you can tell the Republican party that I said so, tell 'em straight from *me*, an' I hain't goin' back on it; I reckon they know who I am, too; I'm a man that's honest — I'm as honest as the day is long, I am — as honest as the day is long — "

He was interrupted by a loud voice. "*Yes*," it cried, "*when that day is the twenty-first of December!*"

That let pandemonium loose again, wilder, madder than before. A member threw a pamphlet at Uncle Billy. In a moment the air was thick with a Brobdingnagian snow-storm: pamphlets, huge wads of foolscap, bills, books, newspapers, waste-baskets went flying at the grotesque target from every quarter of the room. Members "rushed" the old man, hooting, cheering; he was tossed about, half thrown down, bruised, but, clamorous over all other clamours, jumping up and down to shriek over the heads of those who hustled him, his hands waving frantically in the air, his long beard wagging absurdly, still desperately vociferating his Democracy and his honesty.

That was only the beginning. He had, indeed, "found his voice"; for he seldom went now to the boarding-house for his meals, but patronized the free-lunch counter and other allurements of the establishment across the way. Every day he rose in the House to speak, never failing to reach the assertion that he was "as honest as the day is long," which was always greeted in the same way.

For a time he was one of the jokes that lightened the tedious business of law-making, and the members looked forward to his "*Mis-ter Speaker*" as schoolboys look forward to recess. But, after a week, the novelty was gone.

The old man became a bore. The Speaker refused to recognize him, and grew weary of the persistent shrilling. The day came when Uncle Billy was forcibly put into his seat by a disgusted sergeant-at-arms. He was half drunk (as he had come to be most of the time), but this humiliation seemed to pierce the alcoholic vapours that surrounded his always feeble intelligence. He put his hands up to his face and cried like a whimpering child. Then he shuffled out and went back to the saloon. He soon acquired the habit of leaving his seat in the House vacant; he was no longer allowed to make speeches there; he made them in the saloon, to the amusement of the loafers and roughs who infested it. They badgered him, but they let him harangue them, and applauded his rhodomontades.

Hurlbut, passing the place one night at the end of the session, heard the quavering, drunken voice, and paused in the darkness to listen.

"I tell you, fellow-countrymen, I've voted Dem'cratic tick't forty year, live a Dem'crat, die a Dem'crat! An' I'm's honest as day is long!"

. . . .

It was five years after that session, when Hurlbut, now in the national Congress, was called to the district in which Wixinockee lies, to assist his hard-pressed brethren in a campaign. He was driving, one afternoon, to a political meeting in the country, when a recollection came to him and he turned to the committee chairman, who accompanied him, and said:

"Didn't Uncle Billy Rollinson live somewhere near here?"

"Why, yes. You knew him in the legislature, didn't you?"

"A little. Where is he now?"

"Just up ahead here. I'll show you."

They reached the gate of a small, unkempt, weedy graveyard and stopped.

"The inscription on the head-board is more or less amusing," said the chairman, as he got out of the buggy, "considering that he was thought to be pretty crooked, and I seem to remember that he was 'read out of the party,' too. But he wrote the inscription himself, on his death-bed, and his son put it there."

There was a sparse crop of brown grass growing on the grave to which he led his companion.
A cracked wooden head-board, already tilting
rakishly, marked Henry's devotion. It had been
white-washed and the inscription done in black
letters, now partly washed away by the rain, but
still legible:

HERE LIES

THE MORTAL REMAINS

OF

WILLIAM ROLLINSON

A LIFE-LONG

DEMOCRAT

AND

A

MAN

AS HONEST AS THE DAY IS LONG

The chairman laughed. "Don't that beat
thunder? You knew his record in the legislature
didn't you?"

"Yes."

"He *was* as crooked as they say he was, wasn't he ?"

Hurlbut had grown much older in five years, and he was in Congress. He was climbing the ladder, and, to hold the position he had gained, and to insure his continued climbing, he had made some sacrifices within himself by obliging his friends — sacrifices which he did not name.

"I could hardly say," he answered gently, his down-bent eyes fastened on the sparse, brown grass. "It's not for us to judge too much. I believe, maybe, that if he could hear me now, I'd ask his pardon for some things I said to him once."

HECTOR

IT isn't the party manager, you understand, that gets the fame; it's the candidate. The manager tries to keep his candidate in what the newspapers call a "blaze of publicity"; that is, to keep certain spots of him in the blaze, while sometimes it is the fact that a candidate does not know much of what is really going on; he gets all the red fire and sky-rockets, and, in the general dazzle and nervousness, is unconscious of the forces which are to elect or defeat him. Strange as it is, the more glare and conspicuousness he has, the more he usually wants. But the more a working political manager gets, the less he wants. You see, it's a great advantage to keep out of the high lights.

For my part, not even being known or important enough to be named "Dictator," now and then, in the papers, I've had my fun in the game very quietly. Yet I did come pretty near being a famous man once, a good while ago, for about a week. That was just after Hector J. Ransom made his great speech on the "Patriotism of the Pasture" which set the country to talking about him and, in time, brought him all he desired.

You remember what a big stir that speech made, of course — everybody remembers it. The people in his State went just wild with pride, and all over the country the papers had a sort of catch head-line: "Another Daniel Webster Come to Judgment!" When the reporters in my own town found out that Ransom was a second cousin of mine, I was put into a scare-head for the only time in my life. For a week I was a public character and important to other people besides the boys that do the work at primaries. I was interviewed every few minutes; and a reporter got me up one night at half-past twelve to ask for some anecdotes of Hector's "Boyhood Days and Rise to Fame."

I didn't oblige that young man, but I knew enough. I was always fond of my first cousin,

Mary Ransom, Hector's mother; and in the old days I never passed through Greenville, the little town where they lived, without stopping over, a train or two, to visit with her, and I saw plenty of Hector! I never knew a boy that left the other boys to come into the parlour (when there was company) quicker than Hector, and I certainly never saw a boy that "showed off" more. His mother was wrapped up in him; you could see in a minute that she fairly worshipped him; but I don't know, if it hadn't been for Mary, that I'd have praised his recitations and elocution so much, myself.

Mary and I wouldn't any more than get to tell each other how long since we'd heard from Aunt Sue, before Hector would grow uneasy and switch around on the sofa and say: "Ma, I'd rather you wouldn't tell cousin Ben about what happened at the G. A. R. reunion. I don't want to go through all that stuff again."

At that, Mary's eyes would light up and she'd say: "You must, Hector, you must! I want him to hear you do it; he mustn't go away without

that!" Then she'd go on to tell me how Hector
had recited Lincoln's Gettysburg speech at a
meeting of the local post of the G. A. R. and
how he was applauded, and that many of the
veterans had told him if he kept on he'd be Governor of his State some day, and how proud she
was of him and how he was so different from
ordinary boys that she was often anxious about
him. Then she would urge him to let me have
it — and he always would, especially if I said:
"Oh, don't *make* the boy do it, Mary!"

He would stand out in the middle of the floor
and thrust his chin out, knitting his brow and
widening his nostrils, and shout "Of the people,
By the people, and For the people" at the top
of his lungs in that little parlour. He always had
a great talent for mimicry, a talent of which I
think he was absolutely unconscious. He would
give his speeches in exactly the boy-orator style;
that is, he imitated speakers who imitated others
who had heard Daniel Webster. Mary and he,
however, had no idea that he imitated anybody;
they thought it was creative genius.

When he had finished Lincoln, he would say: "Well, I've got another that's a good deal better, but I don't want to go through that to-day; it's too much trouble," with the result that in a few minutes Patrick Henry would take a turn or two in his grave. Hector always placed himself by a table for "Liberty or Death," and barked his knuckles on it for emphasis. Little he cared, so long as he thought he'd got his effect! You could see, in spite of the intensity of his expression, that he was perfectly happy.

When he'd worked us through that, and perhaps "Horatius at the Bridge" and the quarrel scene between Brutus and Cassius and was pretty well emptied, he'd hang about and interrupt in a way that made me restless. Neither Mary nor I could get out two sentences before the boy would cut in with something like: "Don't tell cousin Ben about that day I recited in school; I'm tired of all that guff!"

Then Mary would answer: "It isn't guff, precious. I never was prouder of you in my life." And she'd go on to tell me about another of his triumphs, and how he made up speeches of his own sometimes, and would stand on a box and deliver them to his boy friends, though she didn't say how the boys received them. All the while, Hector would stare at me like a neighbour's cat on your front steps, to see what impression it made on me; and I was conscious that he was sure that I knew he was a wonderful boy. I think he felt that everybody knew it. Hector kind of palled on me.

When he was about sixteen, Mary wrote me that she was in great distress about him because he had decided to go on the stage; that he had written to John McCullough, offering to take the place of leading man in his company to begin with. Mary was sure, she said, that the life of an actor was a hard one; Hector had always been very delicate (I had known him to eat a whole mince pie without apparent distress afterward) and she wanted me to write and urge him to change his mind. She felt sure Mr. McCullough would send for him at once, because Hector had written him that he already knew all the principal Shakespearian rôles, could play Brutus, Cassius, or Mark Antony as desired; and he had added a letter of recommendation from the Mayor of their city, declaring that Hector was a finer elocutionist and tragedian than any actor he had ever seen.

The dear woman's anxiety was needless, for she wrote me, with as much surprise as pleasure, two months later, that for some reason Mr. Mc-Cullough had not answered the letter, and that she was very happy; she had persuaded Hector to go to college.

How she kept him there, the first two years, I don't know, for her husband had only left her about four hundred dollars a year. Of course, living in Greenville isn't expensive, but it does cost something, and I honestly believe Mary came near to living on nothing. It was a small college that she'd sent the boy to, but it was a mother's point with her that Hector should be as comfortable as anyone there.

I stopped off at Greenville, one day, toward the end of his second year, but before he'd come home, and I saw how it was. Mary seemed as glad as ever to see me — it was the same old bright greeting that she'd always given me. She saw me from the dining-room window where she was eating her supper, and she came out, running down to the gate to meet me, like a girl; but she looked thin and pale.

I said I'd go right in and have some supper with her, and at that the roses came back quickly to her cheeks. "No," she said, "I wasn't really at supper; only having a bite beforehand; I'm going up-town now to get the things for supper. You smoke a cigar out on the porch till I get back, and —"

I took her by the arm. "Not much, Mary," I said. "I'm going to have the same supper you had for yourself."

So I went straight out to the dining-room; and all I found on the table was some dry bread toasted and a baked apple without cream or sugar. It gave me a pretty good idea of what the general run of her meals must have been.

I had a long talk with her that night, and I

wormed it out of her that Hector's college expenses were about twenty-five dollars a month, which left her six to live on. The truth is, she didn't have enough to eat, and you could see how happy it made her. She read me a good many of Hector's letters, her voice often trembling with happiness over his triumphs. The letters were long, I'll say that for Hector, which may have been to his credit as a son, or it may have been because he had such an interesting subject. There was no doubt that he had worked hard; he had taken all the chief prizes for oratory and essay writing and so forth that were open to him; he also allowed it to be seen that he was the chief person in the consideration of his class and the fraternity he had joined. Mary had a sort of humbleness about being the mother of such a son.

But I settled one thing with her that night, though I had to hurt her feelings to do it. I owned a couple of small notes which had just fallen due, and I could spare the money. I put it as a loan to Hector himself; he was to pay me back when he got started, and so it was arranged that he could finish his course without his mother's living on apples and toast.

I went over to his Commencement with Mary and we hadn't been in the town an hour before we saw that Hector was the king of the place. He had *all* the honours; first in his class, first in oratory, first in everything; professors and students all kow-towed and sounded the hew-gag before him. Most of Mary's time was put in crying with happiness. As for Hector himself, he had changed in just one way: he no longer looked at people to see his effect on them; he was too confident of it.

His face had grown to be the most determined I have ever seen. There was no obstinacy in it — he wasn't a bull-dog — only set determination. No one could have failed to read in it an immensely powerful will. In a curious way he seemed "on edge" all the time. His nostrils were always distended, the muscles of his lean jaw were never lax, but continually at tension, thrusting the chin forward with his teeth hard together.

His eyebrows were contracted, I think, even in his sleep, and he looked at everything with a sort of quick, fierce appearance of scrutiny, though at that time I imagined that he saw very little. He had a loud, rich voice, his pronunciation was clipped to a deadly distinctness; he was so straight and his head so high in the air that he seemed almost to tilt back. With his tall figure and black hair, he was a boy who would have attracted attention, as they say, in any crowd, so that he might have been taken for a young actor.

His best friend, a kind of Man Friday to him, was another young fellow from Greenville, whose name was Joe Lane. I liked Joe. I'd known him since he was a boy. He was lazy and pleasant-looking, with reddish hair and a drawling, low voice. He had a humorous, sensible expression, though he was dissipated, I'd heard, but very gentle in his manners. I had a talk with him under the trees of the college campus in the moonlight, Commencement night. I can see the boy lying there now, sprawling on the grass with a cigar in his mouth.

"Hector's done well," I said.

"Oh, Lord, yes!" Joe answered. "He always will. He's going 'way up in the world."

"What makes you think so?"

"Because he's so sure of it. It only needs a little luck to make him a great man. In fact, he already is a great man."

"You mean you think he has a great mind?"

"Why, no, sir; but I think he has a purpose so big and so set, that it might be called great, and it will make him great."

"What purpose?"

Joe answered quietly but very slowly, pulling at his cigar after each syllable: "Hec — tor — J. Ran — som!"

"I declare," I put in, "I thought you were his friend!"

"So I am," the young fellow returned. "Friend, admirer, and doer-in-ordinary to Hector J. Ransom, that's my quality. I've done errands and odd jobs for him all my life. Most people who meet him do; though it might be hard to say why. I haven't hitched my wagon to a star; nobody'll get to do that, because this star isn't going to take anything to the zenith but itself."

"Going to the zenith, is he?"

"Surely."

"You mean," said I, "that he's going to make a fine lawyer?"

"Oh, no, I think not. He might have been called one in the last generation, but, as I understand it, nowadays a lawyer has to work out business propositions more than oratory."

"And you think Hector has only his oratory?"

"I think that's his vehicle; it's his racing sulky and he'll drive it pretty hard. We're good friends, but if you want me to be frank, I should say that he'd drive on over my dead body if it lay in the road to where he was going." Lane rolled over in the grass with a little chuckle. "Of course," he went on, "I talk about him this way because I know what you've done for him and I'd like to help you to be sure that he's going to be a success. He'll do you credit!"

"What are you going to do, yourself, Joe?" I asked.

"Me?" He sat up, looking surprised. "Why, didn't you know? I didn't get my degree. They threw me out at the eleventh hour for getting too publicly tight — celebrating Hector's winning the works of Lord Byron, the prize in the senior debate! I'll never be a credit to anybody; and as for what I'm going to do — go back to Greenville and loaf in Tim's pool-room, I suppose, and watch Hector's balloon."

However, Hector's balloon seemed uninclined to soar, at the set-off — though Hector didn't. The next summer began a presidential campaign, and Hector, knowing that I was chairman of my county committee, and strangely overestimating my importance, came up to see me: he asked me to use my influence with the National Committee to have him sent to make speeches in one of the doubtful States; he thought he could carry it for us. I explained that I had no wires leading up so far as the National Committee. There were other things I might have explained, but it didn't seem much use. Hector would have thought I wanted to "keep him down."

He thought so anyway, because, after a crest-fallen moment, he began to look at me in his fierce eye-to-eye way with what seemed to me a dark suspicion. He came and struck my desk with his clinched fist (he was always strong on that), and exclaimed:

"Then by the eternal gods, if my own flesh and blood won't help me, I'll go to Chicago myself, lay my credentials before the committee, unaided, and wring from them —"

"Hold on, Hector," I said. "Why didn't you say you had credentials? What are they?"

"What are they?" he answered in a rising voice. "You ask me what are my credentials? The credentials of my patriotism, my poverty, and my pride! You ask me for my credentials? The credentials of youth!" (He hit the desk every few words.) "The credentials of enthusiasm! The credentials of strength! You ask for my credentials? The credentials of red blood, of red corpuscles, of young manhood, ripest in the glorious young West! The credentials of vitality! Of virile —"

"Hold on," I said again, but I couldn't stop him. He went on for probably fifteen minutes, pacing the room and gesticulating and thundering at me, though we two were all alone. I felt mighty ridiculous, but, of course, I'd been through much the same thing with one or two candidates and orators before. I thought then that he was practising on me, but I came afterward to see that I was partly wrong. "Oratory" was his only way of expressing himself; he couldn't just *talk*, to save his life. All you could do, when he began, was to sit and take it till he got through, which consumed some valuable time for me that afternoon. I suppose I was profane inside, for having given him that cue with "credentials." Finally I got in a question:

"Why not begin a little more mildly, Hector? Why don't you make some speeches in your own county first?"

"I have consented to make the Fourth of July oration at Greenville," he answered.

Before he could go on, I got up and slapped him on the back. "That's right!" I said. "That's right! Go back and show the home folks what you can do, and I'll come down to hear it!"

And so I did. Mary was, if possible, more flustered and upset than at Hector's Commencement. She and Joe Lane and I had a bench close up to the stand, and on the other side of Mary sat a girl I'd never seen before. Mary introduced me to her in a way that made me risk a guess that Hector liked her more than common. Her name was Laura Rainey, and she'd come to Greenville, a year before, to teach in the high-school. She was young, not quite twenty, I reckoned, and as pretty and dainty a girl as ever I saw; thin and delicate-looking, though not in the sense of poor health; and she struck me as being very sweet and thoughtful. Joe Lane told me, with his little chuckle, that she'd had a good deal of trouble in the school on account of all the older boys falling in love with her.

Something in the way he spoke made me watch Joe, and I was sure if he'd been one of her pupils he wouldn't have lightened her worries much in that direction. He had it himself. I saw

it, or, I should say, I felt it, in spite of his never
seeming to look at her. She looked at him, however, and pretty often, too; and there was a good
deal of interest in her eyes, only it was a sad kind,
which I understood, I thought, when I found
that Joe had been on a long spree and had just
sobered up the day before.

Hector sat above us on the platform, with
the Mayor and the County Judge, and when
the latter introduced him, and the same old
white pitcher and glass of water on a pine table,
the boy came forward with slow and impressive
steps, and, setting his left fist on his hip, allowed
his right arm to hang straight by his side till his
hand rested on the table, like a statesman of the
day standing for a photograph. His brow con-
tained a commanding frown, and he stood for
some moments in that position, while, to my astonishment, the crowd cheered itself hoarse.

There was no mistaking the genuine enthusiasm that he evoked, though I didn't feel it myself. I suppose the only explanation is that
he had a great deal of what is called "mag-

netism." What made it I don't know. He was good-looking enough, with his dark eyes and hair, and white, intense face and black clothes; but there was more in the cheering than appreciation of that. I could not doubt that he produced on the crowd, by his quiet attitude, an apparition of greatness. There was some kind of hypnotism in it, I suppose.

The speech was about what I was looking for: bombastic platitudes delivered with such earnestness and velocity that "every point scored" and the cheering came whenever he wanted it.

For instance: he would retire a few steps toward the rear, and, pointing to the sky, adjure it in a solemn voice which made every one lean forward in a dead hush:

"Tell me, ye silent stars, that seem to slumber 'neath the auroral coverlet of day, tell me, down what laurelled pathways among ye walk our dead, the heroes whose blood was our benison, bequeathing to us the heritage of this flower-strewn land; they who have passed to that bourne whence no traveller returns? Answer me: Are not *theirs* the loftiest names inscribed on your marble catalogues of the nations?" He let his voice out startlingly and shouted: "CREEPS there a creature of the earth with spirit so sordid as to doubt it, to doubt *who* heads those gilded rolls! If there be, then *I* say to him, 'Beware!' For the names I see written above me to-day on the immemorial canopy of heaven begin with that of the spotless knight, the unsceptred and uncrowned king, the godlike and immaculate"— (here he turned suddenly, ran to the front of the stage, and, with outstretched fist shaking violently over our heads, thundered at the full power of his lungs): "GEORGE WASHINGTON!"

He did the same for Jefferson, Jackson, Lincoln, Grant, and four or five governors and senators of the State; and at every name the crowd went wild, worked up to it by Hector in the same way. But what surprised me was his daring to conclude his list with a votive offering laid at the feet of Passley Trimmer. Trimmer was the congressional representative of that district and one of the meanest men and smartest politicians in the world. He was always creeping out of tight places and money-scandals by the skin of his teeth; and yet, by building up the finest personal machine in the State, he stuck to his seat in Congress term after term, in spite of the fact that most of the intelligent and honest men in his district despised him. It was a proof of the power Hector held over his audience that, by his tribute to Trimmer, he was able to evoke the noisiest enthusiasm of the afternoon.

Nevertheless, what really tickled me most was the boy's peroration. It gave me a pretty clear insight into his "innard workings." He led up to it in his favourite way: stepping backward a pace or two and sinking his voice to a kind of Edwin Booth quiet; gradually growing a little louder; then suddenly turning on the thunder and running forward.

"You ask *me* for our credentials?" he roared. (Nobody had, this time.) "In the Lexicon of the Peoples, you ask *me* for my country's credentials? The credentials of our pastures, our population and our pride! You ask me for my country's credentials? I reply: 'The credentials of our youth and our enthusiasm! Of red corpuscles! Of red blood! The credentials of the virility and of the magnificent manhood of the Columbian Continent!' You ask for my country's credentials and I answer: 'The credentials of Glory! By right of the eternal and Almighty God!'"

Of course there was a great deal more, but that's enough to show how he had polished it.

I walked back to Mary's with Joe Lane, while Hector followed, making a kind of Royal Progress through the crowds, with his mother and Miss Rainey.

"You see it now, yourself, don't you?" Joe said to me.

"You mean about his doing well?"

"What else? He's just shown what he can do with people. The day will come when you'll have to take him at his own valuation."

I couldn't help laughing. "Well, Joe," I said, "that sounds as if *you*, at least, already took Hector at his own valuation."

"In some things," he answered, "I think I do. Don't you take him for an ass, sir. Sometimes I believe he's guided by a really superior intelligence —"

"Must be a sub-consciousness, then, Joe!"

"Exactly," he said seriously. "He doesn't make a single mistake. He's trained his manner so that, while a very few people laugh at him, he does things that the town would resent in any one else. He doesn't go round with the boys, and they look up to him for it. He isn't pompous, but he's acquired a kind of stateliness of manner that's made Greenville call him 'Mister Ransom' instead of 'Hec.' You probably think that his request to the National Committee only shows he's got all the nerve in the world; but I believe, on my soul, that if it had been granted he could have made good."

"What did he want to run Passley Trimmer into his Pantheon for, to-day?" I asked.

Joe's honest face looked a little dark at this. "It's only another proof of the shrewdness that directs him, though it was, maybe, a little bit sickening. He talks gold and stars and eternal gods, about sweetness and light and pure politics and reform, but he wants Passley Trimmer's machine to take him up. Passley Trimmer and his brother, Link, are a good-sized curse to this district, I expect you know, but Hector's courting them. Link is the dirtiest we've ever had here, and he holds all the rottenest in this county solid for Passley He's overbearing; ugly, too; shot a nigger in the hip a year ago, and crippled him for life on account of a little back-talk, and got off scot-free. I had a row with him in a saloon last week; I was tight, I suppose, though there's always been bad blood between us, anyway, drunk or sober, and I didn't know much what happened, except that I refused to drink in his company and he cursed me out and I blacked an eye for him before they separated us. Well, sir, next day, here was Hector demanding that I go and apologize to Link. I said I'd as soon apologize to a rattlesnake, and Hector upbraided me in his rhetoric, but with a whole lot of real feeling, too. He was even pathetic about it: put it on the ground

that I owed it to morality, by which he meant
Hector. I was known to be his most intimate
friend; I had done him an irrecoverable injury
with the Trimmers, who would extend their re-
taliation and let *him* have a share of it, as my
friend. He ended by declaring that he should
withhold the light of his countenance from me
until I had repaired the wrong done to his cause,
and had apologized to Link!''

"Did you do it?"

The good fellow answered with his little
chuckle: "Of course! Don't you see that he
gets everybody to do what he wants? It's almost
sheer will, and he's a true cloud-compeller."

I wanted to understand something else, and
I didn't know how much Mary could tell me; that
is, I was sure that she would think that Miss
Rainey was in love with Hector. Mary wouldn't
be able to see how any girl could help it.

"Joe," I said, "does Hector seem much taken
with this Miss Rainey?"

We had come to the gate, and Lane stopped
to relight a cigar before he answered. He kept the

match at the stub until it burned out, half hiding his face from me with his hands, shielding the flame from a breeze that wasn't blowing.

"Yes," he said finally, "as much as he could be with anybody — at least he wants her to be taken with him."

"Do you think she is?"

He swung the gate open, and stood to let me pass in first. "She could be of great help to him. We've all got to help Hector."

I was going on: "You believe she will —"

"Did you ever hear," he interrupted, "of Jane Welsh Carlyle?"

I thought about that answer of Joe's most of the evening, and it struck me he was right. It was one of those things you couldn't possibly explain to save your life, but you knew it: everybody had *got* to help Hector. Everybody had to get behind him and push. Hector took it for granted in a way that passed the love of woman!

And yet, as we sat at Mary's supper-table, that evening, I don't know that I ever felt less real liking for any of my kin than I felt for Hector, though, perhaps, that was because he seemed to keep rubbing it in on me in indirect ways that I had done him an injury by not helping him with the National Committee, and that I ought to know it, after his triumph of the afternoon. I could see that Mary agreed with him, though in her gentle way.

Young Lane and Miss Rainey stayed for supper, too, and were very quiet. Miss Rainey struck me as a quiet girl generally, and Joe never talked, anyway, when in Hector's company. For that matter, nobody else did; there was mighty little chance. The truth is, Hector had an impediment of speech: he couldn't listen.

Of course he talked only about himself. That followed, because it was all there was in him. Not that it always *seemed* to be about himself. For instance, I remember one of his ways of rubbing it into me, that evening. He had been delivering himself of some opinions on the nature of Genius, fragments (like his "credentials"— I had a sneaking idea) of some undeveloped oration or other. "Look at Napoleon!" he bade us, while Mary was cutting the pie. "Could Barras with all his jealous and malevolent opposition, could Barras with all his craft, all his machinations, with all the machinery of the State, could Barras oppose the upward flight of that mighty spirit? No! Barras, who should have been the faithful friend, the helper, the disciple and believer, Barras, I say, set himself to destroy the youth whose genius he denied, and Barras was himself destroyed! He fell, for he had dared to oppose the path of one of the eternal stars!"

That was a sample, and I don't exaggerate it. I couldn't exaggerate Hector; it's beyond me; he always exaggerated himself beyond anybody else's power to do it. But I loved to hear Joe Lane's chuckle and I got one out of him when I offered him a cigar as we went out on the porch.

"Take one," I said. "It's one of Barras's best."

"Better get in line," was all he added to the chuckle.

A good many visitors dropped in, during the evening, Greenville's greatest come to congratulate Hector on the speech. Everybody in the county was talking about him that night, they said. Hector received these people in his old-fashioned-statesman manner, though I noticed that already he shook hands like a candidate. He would grasp the caller's hand quickly and decidedly, instead of letting the other do the gripping. And I could see that all those who came in, even hard-headed men twice his age, treated him deferentially, with the air of intimate respect that he somehow managed to exact from people. Perhaps I don't do him justice: he was a "mighty myster'us" boy!

I sat and smoked, lounging in one of Mary's comfortable porch-chairs. I managed without trouble to be in the background and I couldn't help putting in most of my time studying Joe Lane and Miss Rainey. Those two were sitting on the side-steps of the porch, a little apart from the rest of us — and a little apart from each other, too. Lord knows how you get such strong impressions, but I was very soon perfectly sure that these two young people were in love with each other and that they both knew it, but that they had given each other up. I was sure, too, that they were both under Hector's spell, and preposterous as it may seem, that they were under his *will*, and that Hector's plans included Miss Rainey for himself.

It was a mighty pretty evening; full of flower-smells and breezes from the woods, which began just across the village street. Joe sat in a sort of doubled-up fashion he had, his thin hands clasped like a strap round his knees. She sat straight and trim, both of them looking out toward where the twilight was fading. As the darkness came on I could barely make them out, a couple of quiet shadows, seemingly as far away from the group about the lamp-lit doorway where Hector sat, as if they were alone on big Jupiter who was setting up to be the whole thing, far out yonder in the lonely sky.

By and by, the moon oozed round from behind the house and leaked through the trees and I could see them plainer, two silhouettes against the foliage of some bright lilac-bushes. Joe hadn't budged, but the back of Miss Rainey's head wasn't toward me as it had been before; it was her profile. She was leaning back a little, against a post, and looking at Joe — just looking at him. Neither of them spoke a word the whole time, and somehow I felt they didn't need to, and that what they had to say to each other had never been spoken and never would be. It was mighty pretty — and sad, too.

I felt so sorry for them, but it made me more or less impatient with Hector, and with Joe — especially with Joe, I think. It seemed to me he needn't have taken his temperament so hopelessly. But what's the use of judging? When a man has a temperament like that, people who haven't can't tell what he's got to contend with.

That Fourth of July speech gave Hector his chance. His district managers and the Trimmer faction saw they could use him; and they sent him round stumping the district. Two campaigns later the State Committee was using him, and parts of his speeches were being printed in all the party papers over the State. Locally, I suppose you might say, he had become a famous man; at least he acted like one — not that there was any essential change in him. His style had undergone a large improvement, however; his language was less mixed-up, and he seemed clear-headed enough on "questions of the day," showing himself to be well-informed and of a fine judgment.

In these things I thought I saw the hand of Laura Rainey. The teacher was helping him. The seriousness of his face had increased, he had always entirely lacked humour; yet the spell he managed to cast over his audiences was greater. He never once failed to "get them going," as they say. At twenty-nine he was no longer called "a rising young orator"; no, he was usually introduced as the "Hon. Hector J. Ransom, the Silver-tongued Lochinvar of the West."

Things hadn't changed much at Greenville. Mary had always been so proud of Hector that she hadn't inflated any more on account of his wider successes. She couldn't, because she hadn't any room left for it.

Joe Lane still went on his periodical sprees quite regularly, about one week every three months, and he was the least offensive tippler I ever knew. He came up to the city during one of his lapses, and called at my office. He was dressed with unusual care (he was always a good deal of a dandy), and he did not stagger nor slush his syllables; indeed, the only way I could have told what was the matter with him, at first, was by the solemn preoccupation of his expression. A little black pickaninny followed him, grinning and carrying a big bundle, covered with a new lace window-curtain.

"I am but a bearer of votive flowers," Joe said, bowing. Then turning to the little darky, he waved his hand loftily. "Unveil the offering!"

The pickaninny did so, removing the lace curtain to reveal a shiny new coal-bucket in which was a lump of ice, whereon reposed a pair of white kid gloves and a large wreath of artificial daisies.

"With love," said Joe. "From Hector." And he stalked majestically out.

There was a card on the wreath, which Joe had inscribed: "To announce the betrothal. No regrets."

Sure enough, the next morning I had a letter from Mary, telling me that Hector and Miss Rainey were engaged, that they had been so without announcing it, for several years, and she feared the engagement must last much longer before they could be married. So did I, for all of Hector's glittering had brought him very little money. While he had some law practice, of course it was small, in Greenville, and what he had he neglected. Nor was he a good lawyer. I knew him to be heavily in debt to Lane, whose father had died lately, leaving Joe fairly well off; and I knew also that this debt sat very lightly on Hector. I judged so, because in the matter of the advances I had made for his education, I never heard him refer to them. Probably he forgot all about it, having so many more important things to think of.

Mary was right: it was a very long engagement. It had lasted seven years in all, when Passley Trimmer declared himself a candidate for the nomination for Governor and gave Hector the great chance he had been waiting for. Hector "came out" for Trimmer, and came out strong. He worked for him day and night, and he was one of the best cards in Trimmer's hand.

It was easy enough to understand: Trimmer's nomination would leave his seat in Congress vacant and the Trimmer crowd would throw it to Hector.

You could see that the "young Lochinvar" was really a power, and I think they counted on him almost as much as on the personal machine Trimmer had built up. Most of all, they counted on Hector's speech, nominating Trimmer, to stampede the convention. If it was to be done, Hector was the man to do it. There's no doubt in the world of the extraordinary capacity he had for whirling a crowd along into a kind of insane enthusiasm. He could make his audience enthusiastic about *anything;* he could have brought them to their feet waving and cheering for Ben Butler himself, if he had set out to do it. I believe that most of us who were against Trimmer were more afraid of Hector's stampeding the convention than of Trimmer's machine and all the money he was spending.

I was working all I knew for another man, Henderson, of my county, and our delegation would go into the convention sixty-three solid for Henderson, first, last, and all the time. On that account I had to play Barras again to the young Napoleon. He came to see me, and made one of his orations, imploring me to swing half of our delegation for Trimmer on the first ballot, and all of it on the second.

"But they count on me!" he declaimed. "They count on me to turn you! Is a man to be denied by his own flesh and blood? Are the ties of relationship nothing? Can't you see that my whole future is put in jeopardy by your refusal? Here is my opportunity at last and you endanger it. My marriage and my fortune depend on it; the cup is at my lips. My long years of toil and preparation, the bitter, bitter waiting — are these things to go for nothing? I tell you that if you refuse me you may blast the most sacred hopes that ever dwelt in a human breast!''

I only smoked on, and so he did "the jury pathetic," and he was sincere in it, too.

"Have you no heart?" he inquired, his voice shaking. "Can you think calmly of my mother? Remember the years she has waited to see this recognition come to her son! Am I to go back to her and tell her that your answer was 'No'? I ask you to think of her, I ask you to put self out of your thoughts, to forget your own interests for once, and to think of my mother, waiting in the old home in the quiet village street where you knew her in her bright girlhood. Remember that she awaits your answer; forget *me* if you will, but remember what it means to *her*, I say, and *then* if there is a stone in your breast, instead of a human heart, speak the word 'No'!''

I spoke it, and, as he had to catch his train, he departed more in anger than in sorrow, leaving

me to my conscience, he told me. At the door he
turned.

"I warn you," he said, "that this faction of
yours shall go down to defeat! Trimmer will win
this fight, and I shall take his seat in Congress!
That is my first stepping-stone, and I *will* take
it! I have worked too hard and waited too long,
for such as you to successfully oppose me. I tell
you that we shall meet in the convention, and
you and your machine will be broken! The re-
wards, then, to us, the victors!"

"Why, of course," I said, "if you win."

The Trimmer people were strong with the
State Executive Committee, and, in spite of us,
worked things a good deal their own way. They
took the convention away from the State Capital to Greenville, which was, of course, a great
advantage for Trimmer. The fact is, that most of
the best people in that district didn't like him,
but you know how we all are: he *was* one *of* them,
and as soon as it seemed he had a chance to bea.
men from other parts of the State, they began

to shout themselves black in the face for their own. When I went down there, the day before the convention, the place was one mass of Trimmer flags, banners, badges, transparencies, buttons, and brass bands.

I went around to see Mary right away, and while she wasn't exactly cold to me — the dear woman never could be that to anybody — she was different; her eyes met mine sadly and her old, sweet voice was a little tremulous, as if she were sorry that I had done something wrong.

I didn't stay long. I started back to the Henderson headquarters in the hotel, but on my way I passed a big store-room on a corner of the Square, which Trimmer had fitted up as his own headquarters. There was quite a crowd of the boys going in and out, looking cheerful, fresh cigars in their mouths, and a drink or two inside, band coming down the street, everything the way an old-timer likes to see it.

Passley Trimmer himself came out as I was going by, and with him were his brother, Link, and two or three other men, among them a

weasel-faced little fellow named Hugo Siffles,
who kept a drug-store on the next corner. Hugo
wasn't anybody; nobody ever paid any attention
to him at all; but he was one of those empty-
headed village talkers who are always trying to
look as if they were behind the scenes, always
trying to walk with important people. Everybody
knows them. They whisper to the undertaker at
funerals; and during campaigns they have something confidential to communicate to United
States Senators. They meddle and intrude and
waste as much time for you as they can.

When Trimmer saw me, he held out his hand.
"Hello, Ben! I hear you're not *for* me!" he said
cordially.

"How are you running?" I came back at
him, laughing.

"Oh, we're going to beat you," he answered,
in the same way.

"Well, you'll see a good run, first, I expect!"

He walked along with me, Link and the others
following a little way behind; but Hugo Siffles,
of course, walking with us, partly to listen and

tell at the drug-store later, and partly to look like state secrets.

"Sorry you couldn't see your way to join us," Trimmer said. "But we'll win out all right, anyway. I shouldn't think that would be much of a disappointment to you, though. It will be a great thing for one of your family."

"Oh, yes," I said, "Hector."

Trimmer took on a little of his benevolent statesman's manner, which they nearly all get in time. "I have the greatest confidence in that young man's future," he said. "He may go to the very top. All he needs is money. I speak to you as a relative: he ought to drop that school-teacher and marry a girl with money. He could, easily enough."

That made me a little ugly. "Oh, no," I said. "He can make plenty in Congress outside of his salary, can't he? I understand some of them do."

Of course Trimmer didn't lose his temper; instead, he laughed out loud, and then put his hand on my shoulder.

"Look here," he said. "I'm his friend and

you're his cousin. He's one of my own crowd and I have his best interests at heart. That isn't the girl for him. He tells me that, for a long while, she used to advise him against having too much to do with *me*, until he showed her that winning my influence in his favour was his only chance to rise. Now, if *you* have his best interests at heart, as I have, you'll help persuade him to let her go. Why shouldn't he marry better? She's not so young any longer, and she's pretty much lost her looks. And then, you know people will talk —"

"Talk about what?" I said.

"Well, if he goes to Congress, and, with his prospects, throws himself away on a skinny little old-maid school-teacher in the backwoods, one that he's been making love to for years, they might say almost anything. Why can't he hand her over to Joe Lane? I'm sure —"

"That'll do," I interrupted roughly. "I suppose you've been talking that way to Hector?"

"Why, certainly. I have his best interests at —"

"Good-day, *sir!*" I said, and turned in at the hotel and left him, with Hugo Siffles's little bright pig's eyes peeking at me round Trimmer's shoulder.

Sore enough I was, and cursing Trimmer and Hector in my heart, so that when some one knocked on my door, while I was washing up for supper, I said "Come in!" as if I were telling a dog to get out.

It was Joe Lane and he was pretty drunk. He walked over to the bed and caught himself unsteadily once or twice. I'd never seen him stagger before. He didn't speak until he had sat down on the coverlet; then he shaded his eyes with his hand and stared at me as if he wanted to make sure that it *was* I.

"I've just been down to Hugo Siffles's drugstore," he said, speaking very slowly and carefully, "and Hugo was telling a crowd about a conver — conversation between you and Passley Trimmer. He said Trimmer said Hector Ransom ought to drop Miss Rainey — and 'hand her over to Joe Lane.' Is that true?"

"Yes," I answered. "The beast said that."

"There was more," Joe said heavily. "More that im — implied — might be taken to imply scandal, which I believe Trimmer did not seriously intend — but thought — thought might be used as an argument with Hector to persuade him to jilt her?"

"Yes."

"What was said ex — actly? It is being repeated about town in various forms. I want to know."

Like a fool I told him the whole thing. I didn't think, didn't dream, of course, what was in that poor, drunken, devoted head, and I wanted to blow off my own steam, I was so hot.

He sat very quietly until I had finished; then he took his head in both hands and rocked himself gently to and fro upon the bed, and I saw tears trickling down his cheeks. It was a wretched spectacle in a way, he being drunk and crying like a child, but I don't think I despised him.

"And she so true," he sobbed, "so good, so faithful to him! She's given him her youth, her

whole sweet youth — all of it for him!" He got
to his feet and went to the door.

"Hold on, Joe," I said, "where are you going?"

" 'Nother drink!'" he said, and closed the door
behind him.

After supper I went to work with Henderson
and three or four others in a little back-room in
our headquarters; and we were hard at it when
one of the boys held up his hand and said:
"Listen!"

The sounds of a big disturbance came in
through the open windows: shouting and yelling,
and crowds running in the streets below. The
town had been so noisy all evening that I
thought nothing of it. "It's only some delegation getting in," I said. "Go on with the lists."

But I'd no more than got the words out of my
mouth than the noise rolled into the outer rooms
of our headquarters like a wave, and there was a
violent hammering on the door of our room,
some one calling my name in a loud frightened
voice. I threw open the door and Hugo Siffles fell

in, his pig's eyes starting out of his pale, foolish face.

"Come with me!" he shouted, all in one breath, and laying hold of me by the lapel of my coat, tried to drag me after him. "There's hell to pay! Joe Lane came into Trimmer's headquarters, drunk, twenty minutes ago, and slapped Passley Trimmer's face for what he said to us this afternoon. Link Trimmer came in, a minute later, drunk too, and heard what had happened. He followed Joe to Hodge's saloon and shot him. They've carried him to the drug-store and he's asked to speak to you."

I had the satisfaction of kicking that little cuss through the door ahead of me, though I knew it was myself I ought to have kicked.

It was true that Joe had asked to speak to me, but when I reached the drug-store the doctor wouldn't let me come into the back-room where he lay, so I sat on a stool in the store. They'd turned all the people out, except four or five friends of Joe's; and the glass doors and the windows were solid with flattened faces, some of them coloured by the blue and green lights so that it sickened me, and all staring horribly. After about four years the doctor's assistant came out to get something from a shelf and I jumped at him, getting mighty little satisfaction, you can be sure.

"It seems to be very serious indeed," was all he would say. I knew that for myself, because one of the men in the store had told me that it was in the left side.

Half-an-hour after this — by the clock — the young man came out again and called us in to carry Joe home. It was not more than a hundred yards to the old Lane place, and six of us, walking very slowly, carried him on a cot through the crowd. He was conscious, for he thanked us in a weakish whisper, when we lifted him carefully into his own bed. Then the doctor sent us all out except the assistant, and we went to the front porch and waited, hating the crowd that had lined up against the fence and about the gate. They looked like a lot of buzzards; I couldn't bear the sight of them, so I went back into the little hall and sat down near Joe's door.

After a while the assistant opened the door, holding a glass pitcher in his hand.

"Here," he said, when he saw me, "will you fill this with cold water from the well?"

I took it and hurried out to the kitchen, where four or five people were sitting and glumly whispering around an old coloured woman, Joe's cook, who was crying and rocking herself in a chair. I hushed her up and told her to show me the pump. It was in an orchard behind the house, and was one of those old-fashioned things that sound like a siren whistle with the hiccups.

It took me about five minutes to get the water up, and when I got back to Joe's room, a woman was there with the doctors. It was Miss Rainey. She had her hat off, her sleeves were rolled up and, though her face was the whitest I ever saw, she was cool and steady. It was she who took the water from me at the door.

I heard low voices in the parlour, where a lamp was lit, and I went in there. Mary was sitting on a sofa, with a handkerchief hard against her eyes, and Hector was standing in the middle of the room, saying over and over, "My God!" and shaking. I went to the sofa and sat by Mary with my hand on her shoulder.

"To think of it!" Hector moaned. "To think of its coming at such a time! To think of what it means to me!"

His mother spoke to him from behind her handkerchief: "You mustn't do it; you *can't* Hector — oh, you can't, you *can't*."

For answer he struck himself desperately across the forehead with the palm of his hand.

"What is it," I asked, "that your mother wants you not to do?"

"She wants me to give up Trimmer — to refuse to make the nominating speech for him to-morrow."

"You've *got* to give him up!" cried his mother; and then went on with reiterations as passionate as they were weak and broken in utterance. "You can't make the speech, you can't do it, you *can't* —"

"Then I'm done for!" he said. "Don't you see what a frightful blow this pitiful, drunken folly

of poor Joe's has dealt Trimmer's candidacy?
Don't you see that they rely on me more than
ever, *now*? Are you so blind you don't see that I
am the only man who can save Trimmer the
nomination? If I go back on him now, he's done
for and I'm done for with him! It's my only
chance!"

"No, no," she sobbed, "you'll have other
chances; you'll have plenty of chances, dear;
you're young —"

"My only chance," he went on rapidly, ignor-
ing her, "and if I can carry it through, it will
mean everything to me. The tide's running
strong against Trimmer to-night, and I am the
only man in the world who can turn it the other
way. If I go into the convention for him, faithful
to him, and, out of the highest sense of justice,
explain that, even though Lane has been my
closest friend, he was in the wrong and that —"

Mary rose to her feet and went to her son and
clung to him. "No, no!" she cried; "no, *no!*"

"I've got to!" he said.

"What is that you must do, Hector?" It was

Miss Rainey's voice, and came from just behind me. She was standing in the doorway that led from the hall, and her eyes were glowing with a brilliant, warm light. We all started as she spoke, and I sprang up and turned toward her.

"He's going to get well," she said, understanding me. "They say it is surely so!"

At that Mary ran and threw her arms about her and kissed her — and I came near it! Hector gave a sort of shout of relief and sank into a chair.

"What is that you must do, Hector?" Miss Rainey said again in her steady voice.

"Stick to Trimmer!" he explained. "Don't you see that I must? He needs me now more than ever, and it's my only chance."

Miss Rainey looked at him over Mary's shoulder. She looked at him a long while before she spoke. "You know why Mr. Lane struck that blow?"

"Oh, I suppose so," he answered uneasily. "At least Siffles —"

"Yes," she said. "You know. What are you going to do?'

"The right thing!" Hector rose and walked toward her. "I put right before all. I shall be loyal and I shall be just. It might have been a terribly hard thing to carry through, but, since dear old Joe will recover, I know I can do it."

The girl's eyes widened suddenly, while the warm glow in them flashed into a fiery and profound scrutiny.

"You are going to make the nominating speech," she said. It was not a question but a declaration, in the tone of one to whom he stood wholly revealed.

"Yes," he answered eagerly. "I knew you would see: it's my chance, my whole career —"

But his mother, turning swiftly, put her hand over his mouth, though it was to Miss Rainey that she cried:

"Oh, don't let him say it — he can't; you mustn't let him!"

The girl drew her gently away and put an arm about her, saying: "Do you think *I* could stop him?"

"But do you wish to stop me?" asked Hector

sadly, as he stepped toward her. "Do you set yourself not only in the way of my great chance, but against justice and truth? Don't you see that I must do it?"

"It is your chance — yes. I see the truth, Hector." Her eyes had fallen and she looked at him no more, but, with a little movement away from him, offered her hand to him at arm's length. It was done in a curious way, and he looked perplexed for a second, and then frightened. He dropped her hand, and his lips twitched.

"Laura," he said, and could not go on.

"You must go now," she said to all three of us. "The house should be very quiet. I shall be his nurse, and the doctor will stay all night. Isn't it beautiful that Joe is going to get well!"

She went out quickly, before Hector could detain her, back to the room where Lane was.

There's no need my telling you the details of that convention: Henderson was beaten from the start, and Hector's speech was all that happened. If he hadn't made it, there might have been a consolidation on a dark horse, for feeling was high against Trimmer. It isn't an easy thing to go into a convention with a brother locked up in jail on a charge of attempted murder!

I'll never forget Hector's rising to make that speech. There wasn't any cheering, there was a dead, cold hush. This wasn't because his magnetism had deserted him; indeed, I don't think it had ever before been felt so strongly. He was white as white paper, and his face had a look of suffering; altogether I believe I couldn't give a better notion of him than saying that he somehow made me think of Hamlet.

He began in a very low but very penetrating voice, and I don't think anybody in the farthest corner missed a single clear-cut syllable from the first. As I may have indicated, I had never been a warm admirer of his, but with all my prejudice, I think I admired him when he stood up to his task that day. For the effect he intended, his speech was a masterpiece, no less. I saw it before he had finished three sentences. And he delivered it, knowing that even while he did so he was losing the woman he loved; for Hector did love Laura Rainey, next to himself, and she had been part of his life and necessary to him. But though the heavens fell, he stuck to what he had set out to do, and did it masterfully.

Not that what he said could bear the analysis of a cool mind: nothing that Hector ever did or said has been able to do that. But for the purpose, it was perfect. For once he began at the beginning, without rhetoric, and he made it all the more effective by beginning with himself.

"Doubtless there are many among you who think it strange to see me rise to fulfil the charge with which you know me to be intrusted. My oldest and most intimate friend lies wounded on a bed of suffering, stricken down by the hand of another friend whose heart is in the cause for which I have risen. Therefore, you might well question me; you might well say: 'To whom is your loyalty?' Well might I ask myself that same question. And I will give you my answer: 'There are things beyond the personal friendship of man and man, things greater than

individual differences and individual tragedies,
things as far higher and greater than these as the
skies of God are higher than the roof of a child's
doll-house. These higher things are the good of
the State and the Law of Justice!'"

That brought the first applause; and Trimmer's people, seeing the crowd had taken Hector's point, sprang to their feet and began to
cheer. At a tense moment, such as this, cheering
is often hypnotic, and good managers know how
to make use of it on the floor. The noise grew
thunderous, and when it subsided Hector was
master of the convention. Then, for the first
time, I saw how far he would go — and why. I
had laughed at him all my life, but now I believed there was "something in him," as they
say. The Lord knows what, but it was there; and
as I looked at him and listened it seemed to me
that the world was at his feet.

He was infinitely daring, yet he skirted the
cause of the quarrel with perfect tact: "The mis-
interpretation of a few careless and kindly words,
said in passing, and repeated, with garbling ad-

ditions, to a man who was not himself. . . .
The brooding of a mind most unhappily beset
with alcohol. . . . A blow resented by a too
devoted but too violent kinsman. . . ."

Then, with the greatest skill, and rather
quietly, he passed to a eulogium of Trimmer's
public career, gradually increasing the warmth
of his praise but controlling it as perfectly as he
controlled the enthusiasm and excitement which
followed each of his points. For myself, I only
looked away from him once, and caught a
glimpse of Henderson looking sick.

Hector finished with a great stroke. He went
back to the original theme. "You ask me where
my duty lies!" His great voice rose and rang
through the hall magnificently: "I reply — 'first
to my State and her needs'! Is that answer
enough? If it be necessary that I should answer
for my personal loyalty to one man or another
then I ask *you*: 'Shall it go to the friend who,
without cause, struck the first blow? Shall it go
to that other friend who went out hot-headed
and struck back to avenge a brother's wrongs?

Is it only between these that I — and many of you— are to choose to-day ? Is there not a *third* ?' I tell you that I have chosen, and that my loyalty and all my strength are devoted to that other, to that man who has suffered most of all, to him who received a blow and did not avenge it, because in his greatness he knew that his assailant knew not what he did!"

That carried them off their feet. Hector had turned Trimmer's greatest danger into the means of victory. The Trimmer people led one of those extraordinary hysterical processions round the aisles that you see sometimes in a convention (a thing I never get used to), and it was all Trimmer, or rather, it was all Hector. Trimmer was nominated on the first ballot.

There was a recess, and I hurried out, meaning to slip round to Joe Lane's for a moment to find out how he was. I'd seen the doctor in the morning and he said his patient had passed a good night and that Miss Rainey was still there. "I think she's going to stay," he added, and smiled and shook hands with me.

Joe's old darkey cook let me in, and, after a moment, came to say I might go into Mr. Lane's room; Mr. Lane wanted to see me.

Joe was lying very flat on his back, but with his face turned toward the door, and beside him sat Laura Rainey, their thin hands clasped together. I stopped on the threshold with the door half opened.

"Come in," said Joe weakly. "Hector made it, I'm sure."

"Yes," I answered, and in earnest. "He's a great man."

Joe's face quivered with a pain that did not come from his hurt. "Oh, it's knowing that, that makes me feel like such a scoundrel," he said. "I suppose you've come to congratulate me."

"Yes," I said, "the doctor says it's a wonderful case, and that you're one of the lucky ones with a charmed life, thank God!"

Joe smiled sadly at Miss Rainey. "He hasn't heard," he said. Then she gave me her left hand, not relinquishing Joe's with her right.

"We were married this morning," she said, "just after the convention began."

The tears came into Joe's eyes as she spoke. "It's a shame, isn't it?" he said to me. "You must see it so. And I the kind of man I am, the town drunkard ——"

Then his wife leaned over and kissed his forehead.

"Even so it was right — and so beautiful for me," she said.

PART II.

MRS. PROTHEROE

W HEN Alonzo Rawson took his seat as the Senator from Stackpole in the upper branch of the General Assembly of the State, an expression of pleasure and of greatness appeared to be permanently imprinted upon his countenance. He felt that if he had not quite arrived at all which he meant to make his own, at least he had emerged upon the arena where he was to win it, and he looked about him for a few other strong spirits with whom to construct a focus of power which should control the senate. The young man had not long to look, for within a week after the beginning of the session these others showed themselves to his view, rising above the general level of mediocrity and tim- idity, party-leaders and chiefs of faction, men who were on their feet continually, speaking half-a-dozen times a day, freely and loudly. To

these, and that house at large, he felt it necessary to introduce himself by a speech which must
prove him one of the elect, and he awaited im-
patiently an opening.

Alonzo had no timidity himself. He was not
one of those who first try their voices on motions
to adjourn, written in form and handed out to
novices by presiding officers and leaders. He was
too conscious of his own gifts, and he had been
"accustomed to speaking" ever since his days
in the Stackpole City Seminary. He was under
the impression, also, that his appearance alone
would command attention from his colleagues
and the gallery. He was tall; his hair was long,
with a rich waviness, rippling over both brow and
collar, and he had, by years of endeavour, suc-
ceeded in moulding his features to present an
aspect of stern and thoughtful majesty whenever he "spoke."

The opportunity to show his fellows that new
greatness was among them delayed not over-
long, and Senator Rawson arose, long and bony
in his best clothes, to address the senate with a

huge voice in denunciation of the "Sunday Baseball Bill," then upon second reading. The classi-
cal references, which, as a born orator, he felt it
necessary to introduce, were received with ac-
clamations which the gavel of the Lieutenant-
Governor had no power to still.

"What led to the De-cline and Fall of the
Roman Empire?" he exclaimed. "I await an
answer from the advocates of this *de*-generate
measure! I *demand* an answer from them! Let
me hear from them on *that* subject! Why don't
they speak up? They can't give one. Not because
they ain't familiar with history, no sir! That's
not the reason! It's because they *daren't*, because
their answer would have to go on record *against*
'em! Don't any of you try to raise it against me
that I ain't speakin' to the point, for I tell you
that when you encourage Sunday Baseball, or
any kind of Sabbath-breakin' on Sunday, you're
tryin' to start this State on the downward path
that beset Rome! *I'll* tell you what ruined it. The
Roman Empire started out to be the greatest
nation on earth, and they had a good start, too,

just like the United States has got to-day. *Then*
what happened to 'em ? Why, them old ancient
fellers got more interested in athletic games and
gladiatorial combats and racing and all kinds of
out-door sports, and bettin' on 'em, than they
were in oratory, or literature, or charitable insti-
tutions and good works of all kinds! At first they
were moderate and the country was prosperous.
But six days in the week wouldn't content 'em,
and they went at it all the time, so that at last
they gave up the seventh day to their sports, the
way this bill wants *us* to do, and from that time
on the result was *de*-generacy and *de*-gredation!
You better remember *that* lesson, my friends,
and don't try to sink this State to the level of
Rome!''

When Alonzo Rawson wiped his dampened
brow, and dropped into his chair, he was satisfied to the core of his heart with the effect of his
maiden effort. There was not one eye in the place
that was not fixed upon him and shining with
surprise and delight, while the kindly Lieutenant-
Governor, his face very red, rapped for order.

The young senator across the aisle leaned over and shook Alonzo's hand excitedly.

"That was beautiful, Senator Rawson!" he whispered. "I'm *for* the bill, but I can respect a masterly opponent."

"I thank you, Senator Truslow," Alonzo returned graciously. "I am glad to have your good opinion, Senator."

"You have it, Senator," said Truslow enthusiastically. "I hope you intend to speak often?"

"I do, Senator. I intend to make myself heard," the other answered gravely, "upon all questions of moment."

"You will fill a great place among us, Senator!"

Then Alonzo Rawson wondered if he had not underestimated his neighbour across the aisle; he had formed an opinion of Truslow as one of small account and no power, for he had observed that, although this was Truslow's second term, he had not once demanded recognition nor attempted to take part in a debate. Instead, he seemed to spend most of his

time frittering over some desk work, though now
and then he walked up and down the aisles talking in a low voice to various senators. How such
a man could have been elected at all, Alonzo
failed to understand. Also, Truslow was physically inconsequent, in his colleague's estimation
—"a little insignificant, dudish kind of a man,"
he had thought; one whom he would have darkly
suspected of cigarettes had he not been dumbfounded to behold Truslow smoking an old black
pipe in the lobby. The Senator from Stackpole
had looked over the other's clothes with a dis-
approval that amounted to bitterness. Truslow's
attire reminded him of pictures in New York
magazines, or the dress of boys newly home from
college, he didn't know which, but he did know
that it was contemptible. Consequently, after re-
ceiving the young man's congratulations, Alonzo
was conscious of the keenest surprise at his own
feeling that there might be something in him
after all.

He decided to look him over again, more carefully to take the measure of one who had shown

himself so frankly an admirer. Waiting, therefore, a few moments until he felt sure that Truslow's gaze had ceased to rest upon himself, he
turned to bend a surreptitious but piercing scrutiny upon his neighbour. His glance, however,
sweeping across Truslow's shoulder toward the
face, suddenly encountered another pair of eyes
beyond, so intently fixed upon himself that he
started. The clash was like two search-lights
meeting — and the glorious brown eyes that shot
into Alonzo's were not the eyes of Truslow.

Truslow's desk was upon the outer aisle, and
along the wall were placed comfortable leather
chairs and settees, originally intended for the use
of members of the upper house, but nearly always
occupied by their wives and daughters, or " lady-
lobbyists," or other women spectators. Leaning
back with extraordinary grace, in the chair near-
est Truslow, sat the handsomest woman Alonzo
had ever seen in his life. Her long coat of soft
grey fur was unrecognizable to him in connection
with any familiar breed of squirrel; her broad
flat hat of the same fur was wound with a grey

veil, underneath which her heavy brown hair seemed to exhale a mysterious glow, and never, not even in a lithograph, had he seen features so regular or a skin so clear! And to look into her eyes seemed to Alonzo like diving deep into clear water and turning to stare up at the light.

His own eyes fell first. In the breathless awkwardness that beset him they seemed to stumble shamefully down to his desk, like a country-boy getting back to his seat after a thrashing on the teacher's platform. For the lady's gaze, profoundly liquid as it was, had not been friendly.

Alonzo Rawson had neither the habit of petty analysis, nor the inclination toward it; yet there arose within him a wonder at his own emotion, at its strangeness and the violent reaction of it. A moment ago his soul had been steeped in satisfaction over the figure he had cut with his speech and the extreme enthusiasm which had been accorded it — an extraordinarily pleasant feeling: suddenly this was gone, and in its place he found himself almost choking with a dazed sense of having been scathed, and at the same time understood in a way in which he did not understand himself. And yet — he and this most unusual lady had been so mutually conscious of each other in their mysterious interchange that he felt almost acquainted with her. Why, then, should his head be hot with resentment? Nobody had *said* anything to him!

He seized upon the fattest of the expensive books supplied to him by the State, opened it with emphasis and began not to read it, with abysmal abstraction, tinglingly alert to the circumstance that Truslow was holding a low-toned but lively conversation with the unknown. Her laugh came to him, at once musical, quiet, and of a quality which irritated him into saying bitterly to himself that he guessed there was just as much refinement in Stackpole as there was in the Capital City, and just as many old families! The clerk calling his vote upon the "Baseball Bill" at that moment, he roared "No!" in a tone which was profane. It seemed to him that he was avenging himself upon somebody for something and it gave him a great deal of satisfaction.

He returned immediately to his imitation of
Archimedes, only relaxing the intensity of his
attention to the text (which blurred into jargon
before his fixed gaze) when he heard that light
laugh again. He pursed his lips, looked up at the
ceiling as if slightly puzzled by some profound
question beyond the reach of womankind; solved
it almost immediately, and, setting his hand to
pen and paper, wrote the capital letter "O" several hundred times on note-paper furnished by
the State. So oblivious was he, apparently, to
everything but the question of statecraft which
occupied him, that he did not even look up when
the morning's session was adjourned and the law-
makers began to pass noisily out, until Truslow
stretched an arm across the aisle and touched him
upon the shoulder.

"In a moment, Senator!" answered Alonzo in
his deepest chest tones. He made it a very short
moment, indeed, for he had a wild, breath-taking
suspicion of what was coming.

"I want you to meet Mrs. Protheroe, Senator,"
said Truslow, rising, as Rawson, after folding

his writings with infinite care, placed them in his breast pocket.

"I am pleased to make your acquaintance, ma'am," Alonzo said in a loud, firm voice, as he got to his feet, though the place grew vague about him when the lady stretched a charming, slender, gloved hand to him across Truslow's desk. He gave it several solemn shakes.

"We shouldn't have disturbed you, perhaps?" she asked, smiling radiantly upon him. "You were at some important work, I'm afraid."

He met her eyes again, and their beauty and the thoughtful kindliness of them fairly took his breath. "I am the chairman, ma'am," he replied, swallowing, "of the committee on drains and dikes."

"I knew it was something of great moment," she said gravely, "but I was anxious to tell you that I was interested in your speech."

A few minutes later, without knowing how he had got his hat and coat from the cloak-room, Alonzo Rawson found himself walking slowly through the marble vistas of the State house to

the great outer doors with the lady and Truslow.
They were talking inconsequently of the weather,
and of various legislators, but Alonzo did not
know it. He vaguely formed replies to her questions and he hardly realized what the questions
were; he was too stirringly conscious of the rich
quiet of her voice and of the caress of the grey fur
of her cloak when the back of his hand touched
it — rather accidentally — now and then, as they
moved on together.

It was a cold, quick air to which they emerged
and Alonzo, daring to look at her, found that
she had pulled the veil down over her face, the
colour of which, in the keen wind, was like that
of June roses seen through morning mists. At
the curb a long, low, rakish black motor-car was
in waiting, the driver a mere swaddled cylinder
of fur.

Truslow, opening the little door of the ton-
neau, offered his hand to the lady. "Come over
to the club, Senator, and lunch with me," he said.
"Mrs. Protheroe won't mind dropping us there
on her way."

That was an eerie ride for Alonzo, whose feet were falling upon strange places. His pulses jumped and his eyes swam with the tears of unlawful speed, but his big ungloved hand tingled not with the cold so much as with the touch of that divine grey fur upon his little finger.

"You intend to make many speeches, Mr. Truslow tells me," he heard the rich voice saying.

"Yes ma'am," he summoned himself to answer. "I expect I will. Yes ma'am." He paused, and then repeated, "Yes ma'am."

She looked at him for a moment. "But you will do some work, too, won't you?" she asked slowly.

Her intention in this passed by Alonzo at the time. "Yes ma'am," he answered. "The committee work interests me greatly, especially drains and dikes."

"I have heard," she said, as if searching his opinion, "that almost as much is accomplished in the committee-rooms as on the floor? There — and in the lobby and in the hotels and clubs?"

"I don't have much to do with that!" he returned quickly. "I guess none of them lobbyists will get much out of me! I even sent back all their railroad tickets. They needn't come near me!"

After a pause which she may have filled with unexpressed admiration, she ventured, almost timidly: "Do you remember that it was said that Napoleon once attributed the secret of his power over other men to one quality?"

"I am an admirer of Napoleon," returned the Senator from Stackpole. "I admire all great men."

"He said that he held men by his reserve."

"It can be done," observed Alonzo, and stopped, feeling that it was more reserved to add nothing to the sentence.

"But I suppose that such a policy," she smiled upon him inquiringly, "wouldn't have helped him much with women?"

"No," he agreed immediately. "My opinion is that a man ought to tell a *good* woman everything. What is more sacred than —"

The car, turning a corner much too quickly,

performed a gymnastic squirm about an unexpected street-car and the speech ended in a gasp, as Alonzo, not of his own volition, half rose and pressed his cheek closely against hers. Instantaneous as it was, his heart leaped violently, but not with fear. Could all the things of his life that had seemed beautiful have been compressed into one instant, it would not have brought him even the suggestion of the wild shock of joy of that one, wherein he knew the glamorous perfume of Mrs. Protheroe's brown hair and felt her cold cheek firm against his, with only the grey veil between.

"I'm afraid this driver of mine will kill me some day," she said, laughing and composedly straightening her hat. "Do you care for big machines?"

"Yes ma'am," he answered huskily. "I haven't been in many."

"Then I'll take you again," said Mrs. Protheroe. "If you like I'll come down to the State house and take you out for a run in the country."

"When?" said the lost young man, staring at her with his mouth open. "When?"

"Saturday afternoon if you like. I'll be there at two."

They were in front of the club and Truslow had already jumped out. Mrs. Protheroe gave him her hand and they exchanged a glance significant of something more than a friendly goodbye. Indeed, one might have hazarded that there was something almost businesslike about it. The confused Senator from Stackpole, climbing out reluctantly, observed it not, nor could he have understood, even if he had seen, that delicate signal which passed between his two companions.

When he was upon the ground Mrs. Protheroe extended her hand without speaking, but her lips formed the word, "Saturday." Then she was carried away quickly, while Alonzo, his heart hammering, stood looking after her, born into a strange world, the touch of the grey fur upon his little finger, the odour of her hair faintly about him, one side of his face red, the other pale.

"To-day is Wednesday," he said, half aloud.

"Come on, Senator." Truslow took his arm and turned him toward the club doors.

The other looked upon his new friend vaguely. "Why, I forgot to thank her for the ride," he exclaimed.

"You'll have other chances, Senator," Truslow assured him. "Mrs. Protheroe has a hobby for studying politics and she expects to come down often. She has plenty of time — she's a widow, you know."

"I hope you didn't think," responded Alonzo indignantly, "that I thought she was a married woman!"

After lunch they walked back to the State house together, Truslow regarding his thoughtful companion with sidelong whimsicalness. Mrs. Protheroe's question, suggestive of a difference between work and speechmaking, had recurred to Alonzo, and he had determined to make himself felt, off the floor as well as upon it. He set to this with a fine energy, that afternoon, in his committee-room, and the Senator from Stackpole knew his subject. On drains and dikes he had no equal. He spoke convincingly to his colleagues of the committee upon every bill that was before them, and he compelled their humblest respect. He went earnestly at it, indeed, and sat very late that night, in his room at a near-by boarding house, studying bills, trying to keep his mind upon them and not to think of his strange morning and of Saturday. Finally his neighbour in the next room, Senator Ezra Trumbull, long abed, was awakened by his praying and groaned slightly. Trumbull meant to speak to Rawson about his prayers, for Trumbull was an early one to bed and they woke him every night. The partition was flimsy and Alonzo addressed his Maker in the loud voice of one accustomed to talking across wide out-of-door spaces. Trumbull considered it especially unnecessary in the city; though, as a citizen of a county which loved but little his neighbour's district, he felt that in Stackpole there was good reason for a person to shout his prayers at the top of his voice and even then have small chance to carry through the distance. Still, it was a delicate matter to mention and he put it off from day to day.

Thursday passed slowly for Alonzo Rawson,

nor was his voice lifted in debate. There was little but routine; and the main interest of the chamber was in the lobbying that was being done upon the "Sunday Baseball Bill" which had passed to its third reading and would come up for final disposition within a fortnight. This was the measure which Alonzo had set his heart upon defeating. It was a simple enough bill: it provided, in substance, that baseball might be played on Sunday by professionals in the State capital, which was proud of its league team. Naturally, it was denounced by clergymen, and deputations of ministers and committees from women's religious societies were constantly arriving at the State house to protest against its passage. The Senator from Stackpole reassured all of these with whom he talked, and was one of their staunchest allies and supporters. He was active in leading the wavering among his colleagues, or even the inimical, out to meet and face the deputations. It was in this occupation that he was engaged, on Friday afternoon, when he received a shock.

A committee of women from a church society was waiting in the corridor, and he had rounded-up a reluctant half-dozen senators and led them forth to be interrogated as to their intentions regarding the bill. The committee and the law-makers soon distributed themselves into little argumentative clumps, and Alonzo found him-self in the centre of these, with one of the ladies who had unfortunately — but, in her enthusiasm, without misgivings — begun a reproachful ap-peal to an advocate of the bill whose name was Goldstein.

"Senator Goldstein," she exclaimed, "I could not believe it when I heard that you were in favour of this measure! I have heard my husband speak in the highest terms of your old father. May I ask you what *he* thinks of it? If you voted for the desecration of Sunday by a low baseball game, could you dare go home and face that good old man?"

"Yes, madam," said Goldstein mildly; "we are *both* Jews."

A low laugh rippled out from near-by, and

Alonzo, turning almost violently, beheld his lady of the furs. She was leaning back against a broad pilaster, her hands sweeping the same big coat behind her, her face turned toward him, but her eyes, sparklingly delighted, resting upon Goldstein. Under the broad fur hat she made a picture as enraging, to Alonzo Rawson, as it was bewitching. She appeared not to see him, to be quite unconscious of him — and he believed it. Truslow and five or six members of both houses were about her, and they all seemed to be bending eagerly toward her. Alonzo was furious with her.

Her laugh lingered upon the air for a moment, then her glance swept round the other way, omitting the Senator from Stackpole, who, immediately putting into practice a reserve which would have astonished Napoleon, swung about and quitted the deputation without a word of farewell or explanation. He turned into the cloakroom and paced the floor for three minutes with a malevolence which awed the coloured attendants into not brushing his coat; but, when he returned to the corridor, cautious inquiries addressed to the tobacconist, elicited the information that the handsome lady with Senator Truslow had departed.

Truslow himself had not gone. He was lounging in his seat when Alonzo returned and was genially talkative. The latter refrained from replying in kind, not altogether out of reserve, but more because of a dim suspicion (which rose within him, the third time Truslow called him "Senator" in one sentence) that his first opinion of the young man as a light-minded person might have been correct.

There was no session the following afternoon, but Alonzo watched the street from the windows of his committee-room, which overlooked the splendid breadth of stone steps leading down from the great doors to the pavement. There were some big bookcases in the room, whose glass doors served as mirrors in which he more and more sternly regarded the soft image of an entirely new grey satin tie, while the conviction grew within him that (arguing from her behaviour of the previous day) she would not come, and that the Stackpole girls were nobler by far at heart than many who might wear a king's-ransom's-worth of jewels round their throats at the opera-house in a large city. This sentiment was heartily confirmed by the clock when it marked half-past two. He faced the bookcase doors and struck his breast, his open hand falling across the grey tie with tragic violence; after which, turning for the last time to the windows, he uttered a loud exclamation and, laying hands upon an ulster and a grey felt hat, each as new as the satin tie, ran hurriedly from the room. The black automobile was waiting.

"I thought it possible you might see me from a window," said Mrs. Protheroe as he opened the little door.

"I was just coming out," he returned, gasping for breath. "I thought — from yesterday — you'd probably forgotten."

"Why 'from yesterday'?" she asked.

"I thought — I thought —" He faltered to a stop as the full, glorious sense of her presence overcame him. She wore the same veil.

"You thought I did not see you yesterday in the corridor?"

"I thought you might have acted more — more —"

"More cordially?"

"Well," he said, looking down at his hands, "more like you knew we'd been introduced."

At that she sat silent, looking away from him, and he, daring a quick glance at her, found that he might let his eyes remain upon her face. That was a dangerous place for eyes to rest, yet Alonzo Rawson was anxious for the risk. The car flew along the even asphalt on its way to the country like a wild goose on a long slant of wind, and, with his foolish fury melted inexplicably into honey, Alonzo looked at her — and looked at her — till he would have given an arm for another quick corner and a street-car to send his cheek against that veiled, cold cheek of hers again. It was not until they reached the alternate vacant lots and bleak Queen Anne cottages of the city's ragged edge that she broke the silence.

"You were talking to some one else," she said almost inaudibly.

"Yes ma'am, Goldstein, but —"

"Oh, no!" She turned toward him, lifting her hand. "You were quite the lion among ladies."

"I don't know what you mean, Mrs. Protheroe," he said, truthfully.

"What were you talking to all those women about?"

"It was about the 'Sunday Baseball Bill.'"

"Ah! The bill you attacked in your speech, last Wednesday?"

"Yes ma'am."

"I hear you haven't made any speeches since then," she said indifferently.

"No ma'am," he answered gently. "I kind of got the idea that I'd better lay low for a while, at first, and get in some quiet hard work."

"I understand. You are a man of intensely reserved nature."

"With men," said Alonzo, "I am. With ladies I am not so much so. I think a good woman ought to be told —"

"But you are interested," she interrupted, "in defeating that bill?"

"Yes ma'am," he returned. "It is an iniquitous measure."

"Why?"

"Mrs. Protheroe!" he exclaimed, taken aback. "I thought all the ladies were against it. My own mother wrote to me from Stackpole that she'd rather see me in my grave than votin' for such a bill, and I'd rather see myself there!"

"But are you sure that you understand it?"

"I only know it desecrates the Sabbath. That's enough for me!"

She leaned toward him and his breath came quickly.

"No. You're wrong," she said, and rested the tips of her fingers upon his sleeve.

"I don't understand why — why you say that," he faltered. "It sounds kind of — surprising to me —"

"Listen," she said. "Perhaps Mr. Truslow told you that I am studying such things. I do not want to be an idle woman; I want to be of use to the world, even if it must be only in small ways."

"I think that is a noble ambition!" he exclaimed. "I think all good women ought —"

"Wait," she interrupted gently. "Now, that bill is a worthy one, though it astonishes you to hear me say so. Perhaps you don't understand the conditions. Sunday is the labouring-man's only day of recreation — and what recreation is he offered?"

"He ought to go to church," said Alonzo promptly.

"But the fact is that he doesn't — not often — not at *all* in the afternoon. Wouldn't it be well to give him some wholesome way of employing his Sunday afternoons? This bill provides for just that, and it keeps him away from drinking too, for it forbids the sale of liquor on the grounds."

"Yes, I know," said Alonzo plaintively. "But it ain't *right!* I was raised to respect the Sabbath and —"

"Ah, that's what you should do! You think *I*

could believe in anything that wouldn't make it better and more sacred ?"

"Oh, no, ma'am!" he cried reproachfully. "It's only that I lon't see —"

"I am telling you." She lifted her veil and let him have the full dazzle of her beauty. "Do you know that many thousands of labouring people spend their Sundays drinking and carousing about the low country road-houses because the game is played at such places on Sunday? They go there because they never get a chance to see it played in the city. And don't you understand that there would be no Sunday liquor trade, no working-men poisoning themselves every seventh day in the low groggeries, as hundreds of them do now, if they had something to see that would interest them? — something as wholesome and fine as this sport would be, under the conditions of this bill; something to keep them in the open air, something to bring a little gaiety into their dull lives!" Her voice had grown louder and it shook a little, with a rising emotion, though its sweetness was only the more poignant. "Oh, my dear Senator," she cried, "don't you *see* how wrong you are? Don't you want to *help* these poor people?"

Her fingers, which had tightened upon his sleeve, relaxed and she leaned back, pulling the veil down over her face as if wishing to conceal from him that her lips trembled slightly; then resting her arm upon the leather cushions, she turned her head away from him, staring fixedly into the gaunt beech woods lining the country road along which they were now coursing. For a time she heard nothing from him, and the only sound was the monotonous chug of the machine.

"I suppose you think it rather shocking to hear a woman talking practically of such commonplace things," she said at last, in a cold voice, just loud enough to be heard.

"No ma'am," he said huskily.

"Then what *do* you think?" she cried, turning toward him again with a quick imperious gesture.

"I think I'd better go back to Stackpole," he answered very slowly, "and resign my job. I don't see as I've got any business in the Legislature."

"I don't understand you."

He shook his head mournfully. "It's a simple enough matter. I've studied out a good many bills and talked 'em over and I've picked up some influence and —"

"I know you have." she interrupted eagerly. "Mr. Truslow says that the members of your drains and dikes committee follow your vote on every bill."

"Yes ma'am," said Alonzo Rawson meekly, "but I expect they oughtn't to. I've had a lesson this afternoon."

"You mean to say —"

"I mean that I didn't know what I was doing about that baseball bill. I was just pig-headedly goin' ahead against it, not knowing nothing about the conditions, and it took a lady to show me what they were. I would have done a wrong thing if you hadn't stopped me."

"You mean," she cried, her splendid eyes widening with excitement and delight; "you mean that you — that you —"

"I mean that I will vote for the bill!" He

struck his clenched fist upon his knee. "I come to the Legislature to do *right!*"

"You will, ah, you *will* do right in this!" Mrs. Protheroe thrust up her veil again and her face was flushed and radiant with triumph. "And you'll work, and you'll make a speech for the bill?"

At this the righteous exaltation began rather abruptly to simmer down in the soul of Alonzo Rawson. He saw the consequences of too violently reversing, and knew how difficult they might be to face.

"Well, not — not exactly," he said weakly. "I expect our best plan would be for me to lay kind of low and not say any more about the bill at all. Of course, I'll quit workin' against it; and on the roll-call I'll edge up close to the clerk and say 'Aye' so that only him'll hear me. That's done every day — and I — well, I don't just exactly like to come out too publicly for it, after my speech and all I've done against it."

She looked at him sharply for a short second,

and then offered him her hand and said: "Let's shake hands *now*, on the vote. Think what a triumph it is for me to know that I helped to show you the right."

"Yes ma'am," he answered confusedly, too much occupied with shaking her hand to know what he said. She spoke one word in an undertone to the driver and the machine took the very shortest way back to the city.

After this excursion, several days passed, before Mrs. Protheroe came to the State house again. Rawson was bending over the desk of Senator Josephus Battle, the white-bearded leader of the opposition to the "Sunday Baseball Bill," and was explaining to him the intricacies of a certain drainage measure, when Battle, whose attention had wandered, plucked his sleeve and whispered:

"If you want to see a mighty pretty woman that's doin' no good here, look behind you, over there in the chair by the big fireplace at the back of the room."

Alonzo looked.

It was she whose counterpart had been in his dream's eye every moment of the dragging days which had been vacant of her living presence. A number of his colleagues were hanging over her almost idiotically; her face was gay and her voice came to his ears, as he turned, with the accent of her cadenced laughter running through her talk like a chime of tiny bells flitting through a strain of music.

"This is the third time she's been here," said Battle, rubbing his beard the wrong way. "She's lobbyin' for that infernal Sabbath-Desecration bill, but we'll beat her, my son."

"Have you made her acquaintance, Senator?" asked Alonzo stiffly.

"No, sir, and I don't want to. But I knew her father — the slickest old beat and the smoothest talker that ever waltzed up the pike. She married rich; her husband left her a lot of real estate around here, but she spends most of her time away. Whatever struck her to come down and lobby for that bill I don't know *yet* — but I will! Truslow's helping her to help himself; he's got stock in the company that runs the baseball team, but what she's up to — well, I'll bet there's a nigger in the woodpile *some*where!"

"I expect there's a lot of talk like that!" said Alonzo, red with anger, and taking up his papers abruptly.

"Yes, *sir!*" said Battle emphatically, utterly misunderstanding the other's tone and manner. "Don't you worry, my son. We'll kill that venomous bill right here in this chamber! We'll kill it so dead that it won't make one flop after the axe hits it. You and me and some others'll tend to *that !* Let her work that pretty face and those eyes of hers all she wants to! I'm keepin' a little lookout, too — and I'll — "

He broke off, for the angry and perturbed Alonzo had left him and gone to his own desk. Battle, slightly surprised, rubbed his beard the wrong way and sauntered out to the lobby to muse over a cigar. Alonzo, loathing Battle with a great loathing, formed bitter phrases concerning that vicious-minded old gentleman, while for a moment he affected to be setting his desk in order. Then he walked slowly up the aisle, conscious of a roaring in his ears (though not aware how red they were) as he approached the semicircle about her.

He paused within three feet of her in a sudden panic of timidity, and then, to his consternation, she looked him squarely in the face, over the shoulders of two of the group, and the only sign of recognition that she exhibited was a slight frown of unmistakable repulsion, which appeared between her handsome eyebrows.

It was very swift; only Alonzo saw it; the others had no eyes for anything but her, and were not aware of his presence behind them, for she did not even pause in what she was saying.

Alonzo walked slowly away with the wormwood in his heart. He had not grown up among the young people of Stackpole without similar experiences, but it had been his youthful boast that no girl had ever "stopped speaking" to him without reason, or "cut a dance" with him and afterward found opportunity to repeat the indignity.

"What have I *done* to *her?*" was perhaps the hottest cry of his soul, for the mystery was as great as the sting of it.

It was no balm upon that sting to see her pass him at the top of the outer steps, half an hour later, on the arm of that one of his colleagues who had been called the "best-dressed man in the Legislature." She swept by him without a sign, laughing that same laugh at some sally of her escort, and they got into the black automobile together and were whirled away and out of sight by the impassive bundle of furs that manipulated the wheel.

For the rest of that afternoon and the whole of that night no man, woman, or child heard the voice of Alonzo Rawson, for he spoke to none. He came not to the evening meal, nor was he seen by any who had his acquaintance. He entered his room at about midnight, and Trumbull was awakened by his neighbour's overturning a chair. No match was struck, however, and Trumbull was relieved to think that the Senator from Stackpole intended going directly to bed without

troubling to light the gas, and that his prayers
would soon be over. Such was not the case, for no
other sound came from the room, nor were Alonzo's prayers uttered that night, though the unhappy statesman in the next apartment could not
get to sleep for several hours on account of his
nervous expectancy of them.

After this, as the day approached upon which
hung the fate of the bill which Mr. Josephus
Battle was fighting, Mrs. Protheroe came to the
Senate Chamber nearly every morning and afternoon. Not once did she appear to be conscious of
Alonzo Rawson's presence, nor once did he allow
his eyes to delay upon her, though it cannot be
truthfully said that he did not always know when
she came, when she left, and with whom she stood
or sat or talked. He evaded all mention or discus-
sion of the bill or of Mrs. Protheroe; avoided Truslow (who, strangely enough, was avoiding *him*)
and, spending upon drains and dikes all the energy
that he could manage to concentrate, burned the
midnight oil and rubbed salt into his wounds to
such marked effect that by the evening of the

Governor's Reception — upon the morning following which the mooted bill was to come up — he offered an impression so haggard and worn that an actor might have studied him for a make-up as a young statesman going into a decline.

Nevertheless, he dressed with great care and bitterness, and placed the fragrant blossom of a geranium — taken from a plant belonging to his landlady — in the lapel of his long coat before he set out.

And yet, when he came down the Governor's broad stairs, and wandered through the big rooms, with the glare of lights above him and the shouting of the guests ringing in his ears, a sense of emptiness beset him; the crowded place seemed vacant and without meaning. Even the noise sounded hollow and remote — and why had he bothered about the geranium? He hated her and would never look at her again — but why was she not there?

By-and-by, he found himself standing against a wall, where he had been pushed by the press of people. He was wondering drearily what he

was to do with a clean plate and a napkin
which a courteous negro had handed him, half-
an-hour earlier, when he felt a quick jerk at
his sleeve. It was Truslow, who had worked
his way along the wall and who now, standing
on tiptoe, spoke rapidly but cautiously, close to
his ear.

"Senator, be quick," he said sharply, at the
same time alert to see that they were unobserved.
"Mrs. Protheroe wants to speak to you at once.
You'll find her near the big palms under the
stairway in the hall."

He was gone — he had wormed his way half
across the room — before the other, in his simple
amazement could answer. When Alonzo at last
found a word, it was only a monosyllable, which,
with his accompanying action, left a matron of
years, who was at that moment being pressed
fondly to his side, in a state of mind almost as
dumbfounded as his own. "*Here!*" was all he
said as he pressed the plate and napkin into her
hand and departed forcibly for the hall, leaving a
spectacular wreckage of trains behind him.

The upward flight of the stairway left a space underneath, upon which, as it was screened (save for a narrow entrance) by a thicket of palms, the crowd had not encroached. Here were placed a divan and a couple of chairs; there was shade from the glare of gas, and the light was dim and cool. Mrs. Protheroe had risen from the divan when Alonzo entered this grotto, and stood waiting for him.

He stopped in the green entrance-way with a quick exclamation.

She did not seem the same woman who had put such slights upon him, this tall, white vision of silk, with the summery scarf falling from her shoulders. His great wrath melted at the sight of her; the pain of his racked pride, which had been so hot in his breast, gave way to a species of fear. She seemed not a human being, but a bright spirit of beauty and goodness who stood before him, extending two fine arms to him in long, white gloves.

She left him to his trance for a moment, then seized both his hands in hers and cried to him in her rapturous, low voice: "Ah, Senator, you have come! I *knew* you understood!"

"Yes ma'am," he whispered chokily.

She drew him to one of the chairs and sank gracefully down upon the divan near him.

"Mr. Truslow was so afraid you wouldn't," she went on rapidly, "but I was sure. You see I didn't want anybody to suspect that I had any influence with you. I didn't want them to know, even, that I'd talked to you. It all came to me after the first day that we met. You see I've believed in you, in your power and in your reserve, from the first. I want all that you do to seem to come from yourself and not from me or any one else. Oh, I *believe* in great, strong men who stand upon their own feet and conquer the world for themselves! That's *your* way, Senator Rawson. So, you see, as they think I'm lobbying for the bill, I wanted them to believe that your speech for it to-morrow comes from your own great, strong mind and heart and your sense of right, and not from any suggestion of mine."

"My speech!" he stammered.

"Oh, I know," she cried; "I know you think I
don't believe much in speeches, and I don't or-
dinarily, but a few, simple, straightforward and
vigorous words from you, to-morrow, may carry
the bill through. You've made such *progress*,
you've been so *reserved*, that you'll carry great
weight — and there are three votes of the drains
and dikes that are against us now, but will follow yours absolutely. Do you think I would have
' cut' *you* if it hadn't been *best?*"

"But I — "

"Oh, I know you didn't actually promise me
to speak, that day. But I knew you would when
the time came! I knew that a man of power goes
over *all* obstacles, once his sense of *right* is arous-
ed! I *knew* — I never doubted it, that once *you*
felt a thing to be right you would strike for it,
with all your great strength — at all costs — at
all — "

"I can't — I — I — can't!" he whispered
nervously. "Don't you see — don't you see —
I — "

She leaned toward him, lifting her face close to

his. She was so near him that the faint odour of her hair came to him again, and once more the unfortunate Senator from Stackpole risked a meeting of his eyes with hers, and saw the light shining far down in their depths.

At this moment the shadow of a portly man who was stroking his beard the wrong way projected itself upon them from the narrow, green entrance to the grotto. Neither of them perceived it.

Senator Josephus Battle passed on, but when Alonzo Rawson emerged, a few moments later, he was pledged to utter a few simple, straightforward and vigorous words in favour of the bill. And — let the shame fall upon the head of the scribe who tells it — he had kissed Mrs. Protheroe!

The fight upon the "Sunday Baseball Bill," the next morning, was the warmest of that part of the session, though for a while the reporters were disappointed. They were waiting for Senator Battle, who was famous among them for the vituperative vigour of his attacks and for the kind

of personalities which made valuable copy. And
yet, until the debate was almost over, he content-
ed himself with going quietly up and down
the aisles, whispering to the occupants of the
desks, and writing and sending a multitude of
notes to his colleagues. Meanwhile, the orators
upon both sides harangued their fellows, the
lobby, the unpolitical audience, and the patient
presiding officer to no effect, so far as votes went.
The general impression was that the bill would
pass.

Alonzo Rawson sat, bent over his desk, his
eyes fixed with gentle steadiness upon Mrs.
Protheroe, who occupied the chair wherein he
had first seen her. A senator of the opposition
was finishing his denunciation, when she turned
and nodded almost imperceptibly to the young
man.

He gave her one last look of pathetic tender-
ness and rose.

"The Senator from Stackpole!"

"I want," Alonzo began, in his big voice: "I
want to say a few simple, straightforward but

vigorous words about this bill. You may remember I spoke against it on its second reading —"

"You did *that!*" shouted Senator Battle suddenly.

"I want to say now," the Senator from Stackpole continued, "that at that time I hadn't studied the subject sufficiently. I didn't know the conditions of the case, nor the facts, but since then a great light has broke in upon me — "

"I should say it had! I saw it break!" was Senator Battle's second violent interruption.

When order was restored, Alonzo, who had become very pale, summoned his voice again. "I think we'd ought to take into consideration that Sunday is the working-man's only day of recreation and not drive him into low groggeries, but give him a chance in the open air to indulge his love of wholesome sport — "

"Such as the ancient Romans enjoyed!" interposed Battle vindictively.

"No, sir!" Alonzo wheeled upon him, stung to the quick. "Such a sport as free-born Americans and *only* free-born Americans can play in this wide world — the American game of baseball, in which no other nation of the *Earth* is our equal!"

This was a point scored and the cheering lasted two minutes. Then the orator resumed:

"I say: 'Give the working-man a chance!' Is his life a happy one? You know it ain't! Give him his one day. *Don't* spoil it for him with your laws — he's only got one! I'm not goin' to take up any more of your time, but if there's anybody here who thinks my well-considered opinion worth following I say: '*Vote for this bill.*' It is right and virtuous and ennobling, and it ought to be passed! I say: '*Vote for it.*'"

The reporters decided that the Senator from Stackpole had "wakened things up." The gavel rapped a long time before the chamber quieted down, and when it did, Josephus Battle was on his feet and had obtained the recognition of the chair.

"I wish to say, right here," he began, with a rasping leisureliness, "that I hope no member of this honoured body will take my remarks as per-

sonal or unparliamentary — *but*" — he raised a
big forefinger and shook it with menace at the
presiding officer, at the same time suddenly lifting his voice to an unprintable shriek — "I say
to *you*, sir, that the song of the siren has been
heard in the land, and the call of Delilah has been
answered! When the Senator from Stackpole rose
in this chamber, less than three weeks ago, and
denounced this iniquitous measure, I heard him
with pleasure — we *all* heard him with pleasure
— *and* respect! In spite of his youth and the poor
quality of his expression, *we* listened to him. *We*
knew he was sencere! What has caused the
change in him? What *has*, I ask? I shall not tell
you, upon this floor, but I've taken mighty good
care to let most of you know, during the morning, either by word of mouth or by *note* of hand!
Especially those of you of the drains and dikes
and others who might follow this young Samson,
whose locks have been shore! *I've* told you all
about that, and more — *I've* told you the *inside*
history of some *facts* about the bill that I will not
make public, because I am too confident of our

strength to defeat this devilish measure, and prefer to let our vote speak our opinion of it! Let me not detain you longer. *I* thank you!"

Long before he had finished, the Senator from Stackpole was being held down in his chair by Truslow and several senators whose seats were adjacent; and the vote was taken amid an uproar of shouting and confusion. When the clerk managed to proclaim the result over all other noises, the bill was shown to be defeated and "killed," by a majority of five votes.

A few minutes later, Alonzo Rawson, his neckwear disordered and his face white with rage, stumbled out of the great doors upon the trail of Battle, who had quietly hurried away to his hotel for lunch as soon as he had voted.

The black automobile was vanishing round a corner. Truslow stood upon the edge of the pavement staring after it ruefully:

"Where is Mrs. Protheroe?" gasped the Senator from Stackpole.

"She's gone," said the other.

"Gone where?"

"Gone back to Paris. She sails day after to-morrow. She just had time enough to catch her train for New York after waiting to hear how the vote went. She told me to tell you good-bye, and that she was sorry. Don't stare at me Rawson! I guess we're in the same boat! — Where are you going?" he finished abruptly.

Alonzo swung by him and started across the street. "To find Battle!" the hoarse answer came back.

The conquering Josephus was leaning meditatively upon the counter of the cigar-stand of his hotel when Alonzo found him. He took one look at the latter's face and backed to the wall, tightening his grasp upon the heavy-headed ebony cane it was his habit to carry, a habit upon which he now congratulated himself.

But his precautions were needless. Alonzo stopped out of reaching distance.

"You tell me," he said in a breaking voice; "you tell me what you meant about Delilah and sirens and Samsons and inside facts! You tell me!"

"You wild ass of the prairies," said Battle, "I saw you last night behind them pa'ms! But don't you think I told it — or ever will! I just passed the word around that she'd argued you into her way of thinkin', same as she had a good many others. And as for the rest of it, I found out where the nigger in the woodpile was, and I handed that out, too. Don't you take it hard, my son, but I told you her husband left her a good deal of land around here. She owns the ground that they use for the baseball park, and her lease would be worth considerable more if they could have got the right to play on Sundays!"

Senator Trumbull sat up straight, in bed, that night, and, for the first time during his martyrdom, listened with no impatience to the prayer which fell upon his ears.

"O Lord Almighty," through the flimsy partition came the voice of Alonzo Rawson, quaveringly, but with growing strength: "Aid Thou me to see my way more clear! I find it hard to tell right from wrong, and I find myself beset with tangled wires. O God, I feel that I am ignorant, and fall into many devices. These are strange paths wherein Thou hast set my feet, but I feel that through Thy help, and through great anguish, I am learning!"

GREAT MEN'S SONS

Mme. BERNHARDT and M. Coquelin were playing "L'Aiglon." Toward the end of the second act people began to slide down in their seats, shift their elbows, or casually rub their eyes; by the close of the third, most of the taller gentlemen were sitting on the small of their backs with their knees as high as decorum permitted, and many were openly coughing; but when the fourth came to an end, active resistance ceased, hopelessness prevailed, the attitudes were those of the stricken field, and the over-crowded house was like a college chapel during an interminable compulsory lecture. Here and there — but most rarely — one saw an eager woman with bright eyes, head bent forward and body spellbound, still enchantedly following the course of the play. Between the acts the orchestra pattered ragtime and inanities from the new comic operas, while the audience in general took some heart. When the play was over, we were all enthusiastic; though our admiration, however vehement in the words employed to express it, was somewhat subdued as to the accompanying manner, which consisted, mainly, of sighs and resigned murmurs. In the lobby a thin old man with a grizzled chin-beard dropped his hand lightly on my shoulder, and greeted me in a tone of plaintive inquiry:

"Well, son?"

Turning, I recognized a patron of my early youth, in whose woodshed I had smoked my first cigar, an old friend whom I had not seen for years; and to find him there, with his long, dust-coloured coat, his black string tie and rusty hat, brushed on every side by opera cloaks and feathers, was a rich surprise, warming the cockles of my heart. His name is Tom Martin; he lives in a small country town, where he commands the trade in Dry Goods and Men's Clothing; his speech is pitched in a high key, is very slow, sometimes whines faintly; and he always calls me "Son."

"What in the world!" I exclaimed, as we shook hands.

"Well," he drawled, "I dunno why I shouldn't be as meetropolitan as anybody. I come over on the afternoon accommodation for the show. Let's you and me make a night of it. What say, son ?"

"What did you think of the play ?" I asked, as we turned up the street toward the club.

"I think they done it about as well as they could."

"That all ?"

"Well," he rejoined with solemnity, "there was a heap *of* it, wasn't there!"

We talked of other things, then, until such time as we found ourselves seated by a small table at the club, old Tom somewhat uneasily regarding a twisted cigar he was smoking and plainly confounded by the "carbonated" syphon, for which, indeed, he had no use in the world. We had been joined by little Fiderson, the youngest member of the club, whose whole nervous person jerkily sparkled "L'Aiglon" enthusiasm.

"Such an evening!" he cried, in his little spiky voice. "Mr. Martin, it does one good to realize that our country towns are sending representatives to us when we have such things; that they wish to get in touch with what is greatest in Art. They should do it often. To think that a journey of only seventy miles brings into your life the magnificence of Rostand's point of view made living fire by the genius of a Bernhardt and a Coquelin!"

"Yes," said Mr. Martin, with a curious helplessness, after an ensuing pause, which I refused to break, "yes, sir, they seemed to be doing it about as well as they could."

Fiderson gasped slightly. "It was magnificent! Those two great artists! But over all the play — the play! Romance new-born; poesy marching with victorious banners; a great spirit breathing! Like 'Cyrano'—the birth-mark of immortality on this work!"

There was another pause, after which old Tom turned slowly to me, and said: "Homer Tibbs's opened up a cigar-stand at the deepo.

Carries a line of candy, magazines, and fruit, too. "Home's a hustler."

Fiderson passed his hand through his hair.

"That death scene!" he exclaimed at me, giving Martin up as a log accidentally rolled in from the woods. "I thought that after 'Wagram' I could feel nothing more; emotion was exhausted; but then came that magnificent death! It was tragedy made ecstatic; pathos made into music; the grandeur of a gentle spirit, conquered physically but morally unconquerable! Goethe's 'More Light' outshone!"

Old Tom's eyes followed the smoke of his perplexing cigar along its heavy strata in the still air of the room, as he inquired if I remembered Orlando T. Bickner's boy, Mel. I had never heard of him, and said so.

"No, I expect not," rejoined Martin. "Prob'ly you wouldn't; Bickner was Governor along in *my* early days, and I reckon he ain't hardly more than jest a name to you two. But *we* kind of thought he was the biggest man this country had ever seen, or was goin' to see, and he *was* a big

man. He made one president, and could have
been it himself, instead, if he'd be'n willing to
do a kind of underhand trick, but I expect without it he was about as big a man as anybody'd
care to be; Governor, Senator, Secretary of State
— and just owned his party! And, my law! — the
whole earth bowin' down to him; torchlight processions and sky-rockets when he come home in
the night; bands and cannon if his train got in,
daytime; home-folks so proud of him they
couldn't see; everybody's hat off; and all the
most important men in the country following at
his heels — a country, too, that'd put up consider'ble of a comparison with everything Napoleon had when he'd licked 'em all, over
there.

"Of course he had enemies, and, of course,
year by year, they got to be more of 'em, and
they finally downed him for good; and like other
public men so fixed, he didn't live long after
that. He had a son, Melville, mighty likable
young fellow, studyin' law when his paw died. I
was livin' in their town then, and I knowed Mel

Bickner pretty well; he was consider'ble of a man.

"I don't know as I ever heard him speak of that's bein' the reason, but I expect it may've be'n partly in the hope of carryin' out some of his paw's notions, Mel tried hard to git into politics; but the old man's local enemies jumped on every move he made, and his friends wouldn't help any; you can't tell why, except that it generally *is* thataway. Folks always like to laugh at a great man's son and say *he* can't amount to anything. Of course that comes partly from fellows like that ornery little cuss we saw to-night, thinkin' they're a good deal because somebody else done something, and the somebody else happened to be their paw; and the women run after 'em, and they git low-down like he was, and so on."

"Mr. Martin," interrupted Fiderson, with indignation, "will you kindly inform me in what way 'L'Aiglon' was 'low-down'?"

"Well, sir, didn't that huntin'-lodge appointment kind of put you in mind of a camp-meetin' scandal?" returned old Tom quietly. "It did me."

"But —"

"Well, sir, I can't say as I understood the French of it, but I read the book in English before I come up, and it seemed to me he was pretty much of a low-down boy; yet I wanted to see how they'd make him out; hearin' it was thought, the country over, to be such a great *play;* though to tell the truth all I could tell about *that* was that every line seemed to end in 'awze'; and 't they all talked in rhyme, and it did strike me as kind of enervatin' to be expected to believe that people could keep it up that long; and that it wasn't only the boy that never quit on the subject of himself and his folks, but pretty near any of 'em, if he'd git the chanst, did the same thing, so't almost I sort of wondered if Rostand wasn't that kind."

"Go on with Melville Bickner," said I.

"What do you expect," retorted Mr. Martin with a vindictive gleam in his eye, "when you give a man one of these here spiral staircase cigars? Old Peter himself couldn't keep straight along one subject if he tackled a cigar like this. Well, sir, I always thought Mel had a mighty mean time of it. He had to take care of his mother and two sisters, his little brother and an aunt that lived with them; and there was mighty little to do it on; big men don't usually leave much but debts, and in this country, of course, a man can't eat and spend long on his paw's reputation, like that little Dook of Reishtod —"

"I beg to tell you, Mr. Martin —" Fiderson began hotly.

Martin waved his bony hand soothingly.

"Oh, I know; they was money in his mother's family, and they give him his vittles and clothes, and plenty, too. *His* paw didn't leave much either — though he'd stole more than Boss Tweed. I suppose — and, just lookin' at things from the point of what they'd *earned*, his maw's folks had stole a good deal, too; or else you can say they were a kind of public charity; old Metternich, by what I can learn, bein' the only one in the whole possetucky of 'em that really *did* anything to deserve his salary —" Mr. Martin broke off suddenly, observing that I was about to speak, and continued:

"Mel didn't git much law practice, jest about enough to keep the house goin' and pay taxes. He kept workin' for the party jest the same and jest as cheerfully as if it didn't turn him down hard every time he tried to git anything for himself. They lived some ways out from town; and he sold the horses to keep the little brother in school, one winter, and used to walk in to his office and out again, twice a day, over the worst roads in the State, rain or shine, snow, sleet, or wind, without any overcoat; and he got kind of a skimpy, froze-up look to him that lasted clean through summer. He worked like a mule, that boy did, jest barely makin' ends meet. He had to quit runnin' with the girls and goin' to parties and everything like that; and I expect it may have been some hard to do; for if they ever *was* a boy loved to dance and be gay, and up to anything in the line of fun and junketin' round, it was Mel Bickner. He had a laugh

I can hear yet — made you feel friendly to everybody you saw; feel like stoppin' the next man
you met and shakin' hands and havin' a joke
with him.

"Mel was engaged to Jane Grandis when
Governor Bickner died. He had to go and tell
her to take somebody else — it was the only
thing to do. He couldn't give Jane anything but
his poverty, and she wasn't used to it. They say
she offered to come to him anyway, but he
wouldn't hear of it, and no more would he let her
wait for him; told her she mustn't grow into an
old maid, lonely, and still waitin' for the lightning
to strike him — that is, his luck to come; and
actually advised her to take 'Gene Callender,
who'd be'n pressin' pretty close to Mel for her
before the engagement. The boy didn't talk to
her this way with tears in his eyes and mourning
and groaning. No, sir! It was done *cheerful;* and
so much so that Jane never *was* quite sure after-
werds whether Mel wasn't kind of glad to git rid
of her or not. Fact is, they say she quit speakin'
to him. Mel *knowed;* a state of puzzlement or

even a good *mad's* a mighty sight better than
bein' all harrowed up and grief-stricken. And he
never give her — nor any one else — a chanst to
be sorry for him. His maw was the only one heard
him walk the floor nights, and after he found
out she could hear him he walked in his socks.

"Yes, sir! Meet that boy on the street, or go
up in his office, you'd think that he was the gay-
est feller in town. I tell you there wasn't anything pathetic about Mel Bickner! He didn't
believe in it. And at home he had a funny story
every evening of the world, about something
'd happened during the day; and 'd whistle to
the guitar, or git his maw into a game of cards
with his aunt and the girls. Law! that boy didn't
believe in no house of mourning. He'd be up at
four in the morning, hoein' up their old garden;
raised garden-truck for their table, sparrow-
grass and sweet corn — yes, and roses, too; always had the house full of roses in June-time;
never *was* a house sweeter-smellin' to go into.

"Mel was what I call a useful citizen. As I
said, I knowed him well. I don't recollect I ever

heard him speak of himself, nor yet of his father but once — for *that*, I reckon, he jest couldn't; and for himself; I don't believe it ever occurred to him.

"And he was a *smart* boy. Now, you take it, all in all, a boy can't be as smart as Mel was, and work as hard as he did, and not *git* somewhere — in this State, anyway! And so, about the fifth year, things took a sudden change for him; his father's enemies and his own friends, both, had to jest about own they was beat. The crowd that had been running the conventions and keepin' their own men in all the offices, had got to be pretty unpopular, and they had the sense to see that they'd have to branch out and connect up with some mighty good men, jest to keep the party in power. Well, sir, Mel had got to be about the most popular and respected man in the county. Then one day I met him on the street; he was on his way to buy an overcoat, and he was lookin' skimpier and more froze-up and genialer than ever. It was March, and up to jest that time things had be'n hardest of all for Mel. I walked around to the store with him, and he was mighty happy; goin' to send his mother north in the summer, and the girls were goin' to have a party, and Bob, his little brother, could go to the best school in the country in the fall. Things had come his way at last, and that very morning the crowd had called him in and told him they were goin' to run him for county clerk.

"Well, sir, the next evening I heard Mel was sick. Seein' him only the day before on the street, out and well, I didn't think anything of it — thought prob'ly a cold or something like that; but in the morning I heard the doctor said he was likely to die. Of course I couldn't hardly believe it; thing like that never *does* seem possible, but they all said it was true, and there wasn't anybody on the street that day that didn't look blue or talked about anything else. Nobody seemed to know what was the matter with him exactly, and I reckon the doctor did jest the wrong thing for it. Near as I can make out, it was what they call appendicitis nowadays, and had come on him in the night.

"Along in the afternoon I went out there to
see if there was anything I could do. You know
what a house in that condition is like. Old Fes
Bainbridge, who was some sort of a relation, and
me sat on the stairs together outside Mel's room.
We could hear his voice, clear and strong and
hearty as ever. He was out of pain; and he had
to die with the full flush of health and strength on
him, and he knowed it. Not *wantin'* to go,
through the waste and wear of a long sickness,
but with all the ties of life clinchin' him here, and
success jest comin.' We heard him speak of us,
amongst others, old Fes and me; wanted 'em to
be sure not forget to tell me to remember to vote
for Fillmore if the ground-hog saw his shadow
election year, which was an old joke I always
had with him. He was awful worried about his
mother, though he tried not to show it, and
when the minister wanted to pray fer him, we
heard him say, 'No, sir, you pray fer my mamma!' That was the only thing that was different
from his usual way of speakin'; he called his
mother 'mamma,' and he wouldn't let 'em pray

for him neither; not once; all the time he could spare for their prayin' was put in for her.

"He called in old Fes to tell him all about his life insurance. He'd carried a heavy load of it, and it was all paid up; and the sweat it must have took to do it you'd hardly like to think about. He give directions about everything as careful and painstaking as any day of his life. He asked to speak to Fes alone a minute, and later I helped Fes do what he told him. 'Cousin Fes,' he says, 'it's bad weather, but I expect mother'll want all the flowers taken out to the cemetery and you better let her have her way. But there wouldn't be any good of their stayin' there; snowed on, like as not. I wish you'd wait till after she's come away, and git a wagon and take 'em in to the hospital. You can fix up the anchors and so forth so they won't look like funeral flowers.'

"About an hour later his mother broke out with a scream, sobbin' and cryin', and he tried to quiet her by tellin' over one of their old-time family funny stories; it made her worse, so he quit.

'Oh, Mel,' she says, 'you'll be with your father —'

"I don't know as Mel had much of a belief in a hereafter; certainly he wasn't a great church-goer. 'Well,' he says, mighty slow, but hearty and smiling, too, 'if I see father, I — guess — I'll — be — pretty — well — fixed!' Then he jest lay still, tryin' to quiet her and pettin' her head. And so — that's the way he went."

Fiderson made one of his impatient little gestures, but Mr. Martin drowned his first words with a loud fit of coughing.

"Well, sir," he observed, "I read that 'Leglong' book down home; and I heard two or three countries, and especially ourn, had gone middling crazy over it; it seemed kind of funny that *we* should, too, so I thought I better come up and see it for myself, how it *was*, on the stage, where you could *look* at it; and — I expect they done it as well as they could. But when that little boy, that'd always had his board and clothes and education free, saw that he'd jest about talked himself to death, and called for the press notices about his christening to be read to him to soothe his last spasms — why, I wasn't overly put in mind of Melville Bickner."

Mr. Martin's train left for Plattsville at two in the morning. Little Fiderson and I escorted him to the station. As the old fellow waved us good-bye from within the gates, Fiderson turned and said:

"Just the type of sodden-headed old pioneer that you couldn't hope to make understand a beautiful thing like 'L'Aiglon' in a thousand years. I thought it better not to try, didn't you ?"

THE END

Trieste Publishing has a massive catalogue of classic book titles. Our aim is to provide readers with the highest quality reproductions of fiction and non-fiction literature that has stood the test of time. The many thousands of books in our collection have been sourced from libraries and private collections around the world.

The titles that Trieste Publishing has chosen to be part of the collection have been scanned to simulate the original. Our readers see the books the same way that their first readers did decades or a hundred or more years ago. Books from that period are often spoiled by imperfections that did not exist in the original. Imperfections could be in the form of blurred text, photographs, or missing pages. It is highly unlikely that this would occur with one of our books. Our extensive quality control ensures that the readers of Trieste Publishing's books will be delighted with their purchase. Our staff has thoroughly reviewed every page of all the books in the collection, repairing, or if necessary, rejecting titles that are not of the highest quality. This process ensures that the reader of one of Trieste Publishing's titles receives a volume that faithfully reproduces the original, and to the maximum degree possible, gives them the experience of owning the original work.

We pride ourselves on not only creating a pathway to an extensive reservoir of books of the finest quality, but also providing value to every one of our readers. Generally, Trieste books are purchased singly - on demand, however they may also be purchased in bulk. Readers interested in bulk purchases are invited to contact us directly to enquire about our tailored bulk rates. Email: customerservice@triestepublishing.com

You May Also Like

ISBN: 9780649565733
Paperback: 170 pages
Dimensions: 6.14 x 0.36 x 9.21 inches
Language: eng

Longmans' English Classics; Dryden's Palamon and Arcite

William Tenney Brewster

ISBN: 9780649731213
Paperback: 160 pages
Dimensions: 6.14 x 0.34 x 9.21 inches
Language: eng

War Poems, 1898

California Club & Irving M. Scott

You May Also Like

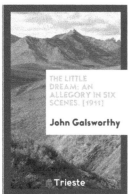

ISBN: 9780649637270
Paperback: 50 pages
Dimensions: 6.14 x 0.10 x 9.21 inches
Language: eng

The Little Dream: An Allegory in Six Scenes. [1911]

John Galsworthy

ISBN: 9780649057054
Paperback: 140 pages
Dimensions: 6.14 x 0.30 x 9.21 inches
Language: eng

The University of Minnesota. The Calendar for the Year 1883-84

University Minneapolis

www.triestepublishing.com

You May Also Like

ISBN: 9780649420544
Paperback: 108 pages
Dimensions: 6.14 x 0.22 x 9.21 inches
Language: eng

1807-1907 The One Hundredth Anniversary of the incorporation of the Town of Arlington Massachusetts

Various

ISBN: 9780649194292
Paperback: 44 pages
Dimensions: 6.14 x 0.09 x 9.21 inches
Language: eng

Biennial report of the Board of State Harbor Commissioners, for the two fiscal years commencing July 1, 1890, and ending June 30, 1892

Various

www.triestepublishing.com

You May Also Like

Biennial report of the Board of State Harbor Commissioners for the two fisca years. Commeneing July 1, 1884, and Ending June 30, 1886

Various

ISBN: 9780649199693
Paperback: 48 pages
Dimensions: 6.14 x 0.10 x 9.21 inches
Language: eng

Biennial report of the Board of state commissioners, for the two fiscal years, commencing July 1, 1890, and ending June 30, 1892

Various

ISBN: 9780649196395
Paperback: 44 pages
Dimensions: 6.14 x 0.09 x 9.21 inches
Language: eng

Find more of our titles on our website. We have a selection of thousands of titles that will interest you. Please visit

www.triestepublishing.com

Lightning Source UK Ltd.
Milton Keynes UK
UKHW02f1841240618
324723UK00010B/357/P